I0636265

TRAIL MIX 2: BEETLE JUICE

TRAIL MIX 2: BEETLE JUICE

PIERS ANTHONY

OPEN ROAD
INTEGRATED MEDIA
NEW YORK

ISBN: 978-1-5040-3953-6

This edition published in 2017 by Open Road Integrated Media, Inc.
180 Maiden Lane
New York, NY 10038
www.openroadmedia.com

TRAIL MIX 2: BEETLE JUICE

CHAPTER 1: HAUNT

———

Wetzel was thinking about the haunted house as he played in the sand. It was some distance away from the village, in an overgrown field, and its roof was sagging down. The children were not allowed to go there. That of course made it fascinating.

Why was it forbidden? What secrets were hidden there? The more he thought about it, the more he had to know. But how could he find out? The adults were always watching, even when they didn't seem to be. They had telepathy they used to spy on children. It was unfair.

A girl came to join him. She was Willa, with blonde corkscrew curls, a pouty mouth, and he didn't really like her though she was the only one whose hair was almost as pale as his tow head. He preferred to play with boys. But she just plumped down before him and started rearranging his sand. He had started a castle with a wall around it; she started another castle, interrupting the wall.

"Your eyes are almost as white as your hair," she said. "Or the sand. I like that."

He saw no reason to be polite. "I don't care."

"There's a way," she murmured.

"I already know how to make a sand castle," he said. "Better than any girl. Go away."

"A way to explore the haunted house."

He stared at her. How had she guessed about that? Yet she had his interest. "What way?"

"At night, when they think we're asleep. They don't watch us then. We can sneak out and see it by moonslight."

"But they're watching us now," he protested.

"No they aren't."

"How can you know that?" Then he caught on. "The telepathy! You have it!"

"Yes. I'm precocious. Don't tell."

Telepathy normally developed at puberty, along with the were forms, but some got it earlier. "I won't," he said, awed.

"I knew I could trust you. There's something about you. Do we have a date?"

Wetzel was wickedly tempted. He knew that two of the four moons would be out this night, doubling the light. It would still be faint, but enough to see by. "Yes. But what if they read our minds?"

"We're just children. They don't bother unless we act funny. They've got better things to do than spy on us. Adult things. So act normal, and don't think about tonight."

"How can I *not* think about it?"

"Think about chocolate cake and ice cream instead."

Wetzel concentrated. "Like this?" He mentally pictured a cake the size of a house, dripping with chocolate sauce.

She licked her lips. "That's it."

That evening when the others slept and the adult proctor was diverted by a book, Wetzel got up, dressed, and snuck out. It was surprisingly easy. The proctor could have caught him any time, but simply didn't expect this, so missed it. Willa was right: adults really didn't pay much attention to behaving children.

Willa met him outside, having sneaked out similarly from the girls' dorm. She took his hand and led him down the street and out of the village. Wetzel was phenomenally excited to be doing this illicit exploration.

"Stop it!" she hissed. "You'll alert them."

The mind reading; he had forgotten. "Chocolate cake and ice cream," he said, focusing.

"That's it. Children are always thinking about things like that."

"But not you?"

"I have other concerns."

"What concerns?"

"You'll see."

He wasn't sure he trusted this. "What concerns?" he repeated, halting his walk.

"Get moving," she said impatiently.

"What if I don't?"

"I'll kiss you."

"Ha."

She stepped close, put her arms around him, and kissed him on the cheek.

"Okay, okay, I'm moving!" he said quickly.

"Worse, you liked it."

"I did not!" But he was lying.

"You forgot again that I can read your mind. But that wasn't my

3

other concern."

"The hunted house!" he said, glad to change the subject. Then, quickly: "Chocolate cake!"

"That too," she agreed.

"You knew I was thinking about it today. That's why you came to my sand lot."

"You're pretty smart, for a boy."

"Thanks," he said dryly.

The moons were indeed bright. They made their way to the lot where the house lurked. There it was, twice as sinister in the half light. Wetzel felt a chill of apprehension.

"Ooh come *on,*" Willa said, forging toward it so that he had to follow. "You know there's no such thing as haunts. Not really."

"How can you be so sure?"

"I read some minds. The adults don't believe in anything supernatural. They've investigated, and know. I have to believe them."

"Maybe they're just thinking it for your benefit, knowing you're peeping."

"No they aren't."

"How do you know?"

"Because I snooped on stuff I *know* they don't want kids to know about."

"Like what?"

"Like breeding."

Well, now. That was an even bigger curiosity than the haunted house. Wetzel, like all children, knew that the adults did it, but none would let a child see it happen, or even describe it to them. Something about a man and a woman, naked, together. The rest was a blank. "You have seen it?"

"Yes, mentally. Keep your thoughts down."

"Chocolate cake," he said, summoning the mental image. "Will you tell me?"

"Soon. First we must explore the house."

Oh. That was why they had come here. At least, it was why he had; he wasn't sure about Willa, since she didn't believe in haunts. "Yes."

They reached the house. It loomed huge, up close, with a big closed front door, smudged windows, and weeds tying to get in under it.

Willa put her hand on the door handle and turned it. She pushed and the door creaked inward to reveal the darkness within. Wetzel felt another thrill of nervousness. Could there really be ghosts?

"Oh, for Peter's sake!" Willa snapped. "Get rational."

"Sorry." Yet it was hard to put aside the phantasms of his fancy. He did not have the reassurance of reading informed adult minds. After all, there must be some reason the house was forbidden to children.

"It's too dark," Willa decided. "I'll light my candle."

"You have a candle?"

"It's called being prepared, dodo." She brought out a dish candle and a flint striker, and in a moment had a spark and a flame.

"Neat," Wetzel said. She obviously did know what she was doing. Too bad she was such a grouch.

"I heard that."

Oops. He wasn't used to having his mind read by a child, especially a nervy girl. Now he had to defend his position. "Well, you are. Why can't you just be smart without being snotty?"

"Oh, and you're smart without being superior?"

Wetzel laughed. "I'm neither smart nor superior. I'm just curious about things."

She softened. "You are smart. Smarter than I am. The adults think so, anyway."

That was a surprise. "They never told me."

She smiled. She was pretty when she did that. Maybe it was the flickering candlelight. "Or me. I snooped it. They think you have great potential. That's why I wanted to get to know you better."

Wetzel was amazed. "So it's not really about the haunted house."

"See? You caught on already."

"Just common sense." But he was pleased, and coming to like her better. Or at least dislike her less.

And of course she knew it. "The time may come when you actually want my favor," she said.

"Never." But his denial lacked force.

They edged in, their eyes adjusting to the interior gloom and the flickering light. The house was empty, with dust layered everywhere. Nobody had been in it for a long time. But of course ghosts wouldn't leave tracks.

"Every time I think you have potential, you get back into that supernatural garbage," she said severely.

"Sorry." He was guilty of that.

Indeed, there was no sign of ghosts or any other supernatural threat. It was just an ordinary deserted house. Wetzel was almost disappointed. The mystery had been more intriguing than the reality.

"But there must be a reason they don't want us here," Willa said.

"And that's what brings you here," Wetzel said. "Not spooks, but the mystery."

"That too," she agreed.

"You said that before."

"It was true before."

Well, she would surely tell him her real reason when she was ready.

"Yes I will."

Damn that telepathy! His mind was an open book to her. Suppose he thought of something naughty, like pooping on the path? She'd know.

Willa giggled. "Yes."

Wetzel suppressed his embarrassment and plowed on. "Maybe there's something in the cellar."

They made their way down the creaky cellar stairs. The cellar was small and lined with stone, evidently serving as a storm shelter in time of need. It was empty.

"Well, that's it," Willa said. "No spooks here. No hidden treasure. It's just an empty house."

"Not worth the risk," Wetzel agreed.

"Fortunately no one knows we're here. There's a faint trace when a person reads your mind, and there's none now."

"There is? I mean, a trace when someone does?"

"Yes. I'll show you. Listen carefully, mentally, and I'll snoop. See if you can feel it."

Wetzel tried to blank his mind. Then he did feel a little odd feathery something, like a soundless whisper. "I got it!"

"Right. You can't tell who, just that someone's there. When you do, you have to quickly do chocolate cake until they stop."

"Wow," he said, awed.

Willa set the candle on the floor between them. "Now we can talk." She sat down on the stone floor, her knees raised.

In that position, her legs showed under her skirt, flickering in the candlelight. Wetzel knew he shouldn't look, but couldn't help himself. Forbidden territory of any type intrigued him. And realized she was reading his mind again. "Sorry."

"I'll show you mine if you show me yours."

He was startled. "What?"

"You heard me."

She knew that he wanted a peek. "But we're not supposed to.

That's why the dorms are separate."

"Precisely. That's why I want to see it."

He was wickedly intrigued, but cautious. "But you've read the minds of adults, so you've seen it already."

"I've seen it in my mind, and felt the huge pleasure they get from it. But that's not the same as seeing it physically. What I've snooped on makes me truly curious to see exactly what's there, so I can know better how it relates."

"That's why you're showing me your legs! You want me to want to see more. So I'll show you mine."

"Precisely. And it's working."

"It's working," he agreed. "Still, we're not supposed to. We could get in trouble."

"Not if we don't tell."

"But they'll read our minds."

"Not if they don't suspect. Think chocolate cake."

Wetzel wasn't sure how well that would work. But his guilty curiosity overwhelmed his caution. "Okay. Who's first?"

"I am, since it's my idea. But you've got to do it too."

"I will." He knew she was reading his sincerity. She had made an impression on him, and now he was committed.

Willa, stood, then drew off her shirt. Her chest was flat like his; no surprise there. Then she stepped out of her shoes, pulled down her skirt and stood in her panties. Wetzel was really excited. He was about to see the secret place of girls.

Then she froze.

"What's the matter?" he asked. Had she lost her nerve?

"Suddenly I know why this house is forbidden," she said.

"Why?"

"Look behind you."

Wetzel turned around and looked at the stairs. There were several mice. "That's nothing. Every house has mice."

"There aren't ordinary. I can read enough of their little minds to know."

Now he saw that the mice were sitting up on their haunches, staring at the two people with uncanny focus. "What are they?"

"Were-mice. Like were-wolves only smaller."

"Were-wolves," he echoed. They were wolves that changed form, just as grown people did. The ability was less common in other animals, but did occur. "But they're not dangerous."

"These are. They change into poisonous snakes, and they don't like us."

"We're in trouble," he breathed.

"I wish I'd picked that up from the adult minds. But they weren't thinking about this place. It's only conscious thoughts that can be read. The rest is an indecipherable tangle." She had adult vocabulary, too.

Wetzel looked around. He saw a loose stone in a corner. He ran to pick it up. "I'll try to fight them off while you escape."

Willa stood nervously close beside him, watching the mice. "You're brave," she said, and kissed him on the cheek. He really liked that, this time, but kept his eyes on the mice.

Now the first one changed. It became a full-sized cobra. Were conversions weren't limited to the size of the original creatures; they could be larger or smaller. What didn't change was the mind: they would be no smarter than mice. But in this situation, mice were plenty smart enough. They probably preyed on larger creatures, when they had the chance. As they did now.

The cobra slithered toward him. Wetzel held his stone, ready to try to bash it on the head when it struck, but he was not at all sure he would be fast enough.

Then he got a notion. Why wait helplessly for it to attack? Why play its game? Better to make it play *his* game.

Except for one thing. "Are they telepathic?"

"Not that I know of. They're *animals*."

"Good. Then I can surprise them. You pick up the candle and use it to stop any snake from approaching you; they'll be fearful of fire."

"Good idea," she agreed, picking up the candle and holding it defensively before her.

Wetzel dived for the snake, and bashed his rock down. On its tail.

The cobra whipped around, striking at him. But Wetzel was already backing away. He had indeed surprised it, and had made the first score.

The snake, injured, did not attack. It transformed back into the mouse. With a bashed tail. It fled.

"You're so brave," Willa repeated.

"I'm not brave! I'm scared."

"That's what bravery is. To be scared, but to do it anyway."

It did not require human intelligence to realize that the prey was fighting back. Three more mice transformed, becoming a copperhead, a cottonmouth, and a rattlesnake. The third one slithered forward.

"I can't get around those," Willa said.

"Maybe you can, if you leap over them when I bash one."

Wetzel oriented on the rattlesnake. He was terrified, but that lent him strength and agility. He could bash its tail. It might bite him, but at least he could make it hurt.

The rattlesnake, seeing his attention on it, stopped. But now the two others advanced, from either side. He turned to face the cottonmouth. It halted, and the rattlesnake resumed its advance.

"They're corralling you," Willa said. "That must be the way they hunt."

"I'll go after the rattler. You jump and run up the stairs."

"I'll try." Then, after a pause, "I think I love you."

Wetzel might have made a smart retort, if he had been able to think of one. If he wasn't remembering that second kiss on the cheek. If he wasn't so distracted by the need to handle the snakes. "Go!" he said, and dived for the rattler, swinging the stone.

Then something else happened. Three larger rodents came scrambling down the stairs. Each oriented on a snake. In moments they had the snakes by the neck and were shaking them to death.

"Mongooses!" Willa said, amazed.

In moments the mongooses transformed to human beings: two men and a woman, members of the village. "Come with us," the woman said severely. Then she paused, looking at Willa. "Put on your clothing."

Wetzel knew the two of them were in serious trouble. They had forgotten to keep their thoughts low; they must have been mentally screaming loudly enough to be heard far away, and the adults had responded.

He dropped the stone. Meekly, Willa dressed, and they went with the woman. The adult said not another word, but her disapproval was like an icy cloud. She merely marched them back to their dorms and let Willa go into hers.

All she said as Wetzel went to his dorm was "Say nothing to anyone."

"Yes, ma'am." Then he was inside, and he hadn't even been missed. He returned to his bed and lay there, shaking. What would happen to him tomorrow?

Finally he slept. What a day it had been!

As it turned out, nothing happened. No one said a word to him. The routine was completely ordinary.

Except for one thing: when they had the common play period with the girls, Willa was not there. She was simply gone. No adult said anything about her absence; it was as if she had ceased to exist. The other children looked a bit nervous, but did not inquire. Neither did Wetzel.

That was the way of it. Wetzel suffered no apparent consequence for his misdeed. It was as if it hadn't happened. Maybe this was the payback for his silence: he would receive no open rebuke as long as he kept his mouth shut.

Willa had paid the price for both of them. Maybe because of her precocious telepathy, an ability that children weren't supposed to have. Maybe because she had undressed most of the way in his presence. Those were the only things he could think of that she had done that he had not. He hated the fact that she was gone, just when he was starting to like her.

He was sure adults were monitoring him telepathically; sometimes he felt the faint traces of their presence, just as Willa had told him. Immediately he thought about chocolate cake. He knew it was all right as long as he was not thinking about the adventure of the night. He trained himself to think of other things. He wasn't sure why, since the adults knew all about the visit to the haunted house, but concluded that if he didn't want to be abruptly disappeared the way Willa had, this was his best course.

However, whatever he managed not to think of, he made sure to stay out of mischief. Maybe he was on probation, and the next offense would get him wiped out. It occurred to him that this could be a very efficient way to make an unruly child behave. Maybe other children had transgressed, and been similarly cautioned, and so no one else knew. It was certainly effective. He was now a good child, perfectly behaved, and he would stay that way.

Then he felt the first touch of telepathy. Not the feather touch of an adult checking his mind; this was his own precocious awareness of the minds of those around him. Their likes and dislikes, their prides and shames, their hopes and fears. All of them very like his own, but *not* his own.

Wetzel froze, mentally. He could not afford this! Discovery would surely banish him, as it had Willa. But what could he do?

He could hide, as he had been doing. Only now he had to make it more effective mentally. Chocolate cake would not be enough; that was merely a noise cover. He needed a place to hide illicit information. He needed his mind to be as innocent and well behaved as his body. But where?

Maybe the haunted house. He was now satisfied that it wasn't haunted, indeed that there were no supernatural spooks, as Willa had believed. But it was forbidden, for good reason: the were-mice lurked there. He would never dare go there again. So it was an ideal hiding place, not physically, but mentally. A place of fear where his thoughts should not go.

He worked on it as quickly as he could, picturing the decrepit house, the dust, the stone cellar, the were-mice, evoking the fear. Here was his storage place for whatever he could not afford to have known. Only he could enter here; fear was a barrier to all others.

Well, not exactly. The adults were not afraid of the were-mice; they could handle them. It was children who were in danger. But if an adult checked Wetzel's mind and felt the fear there, that person would know that this was a memory Wetzel was trying to hide from himself, and would not explore it further. If Wetzel had figured it out correctly.

He worked on his mental refuge, shoring up the fear. Then he did a mental exercise he would never even have thought of before this need arose: he dragged his secrets there. He stacked them in the stone cellar to be guarded by the poisonous snakes. Who would ever find them there?

The biggest secret was hard to drag. That was his dawning telepathy. He couldn't stop it from happening, but he could bury it, keeping it out of his conscious awareness. Then when he went to hide in the cellar himself, he could review what had come in.

The most immediate things were the impressions other children had of him. One boy thought he was too goody-goody. Well, he was, now, deliberately, so the assessment didn't bother him. And there was a vital key: it was not so much the information, but how he felt about it that counted. If he did not react emotionally it was largely invisible.

A girl thought he was cute. That would have been interesting, except that Willa had liked him and almost shown him her secret place, and been severely punished. That made him extremely wary of girls who might have anything similar in mind. So it was easy not to react, which was what counted.

Mostly, the other children found him indifferent, nothing special. Just like themselves. That was exactly how he wanted to be viewed. It was a form of anonymity.

Day by day he perfected his hiding place. The advantage of having it mental was that he could access it at any time, and feed new secrets into it before an adult could snoop. It became almost automatic. On the surface he was the same as he had been. Only down inside the scary cellar of the haunted house was his new status displayed. That was his storm shelter, his one safe place.

It helped that no one was really trying to spy on him. The feather touches were routine, checking him as one of many children, satisfied to find what they expected: a boy who really liked chocolate cake and had little ambition for anything else. His official identity.

Meanwhile the schooling was rigorous. They had to learn every nuance of the language, and master the written form too. They studied the history of their species, which was like none other known: telepathic weres with divergent forms. Wetzel's favorite teacher, Weava, was a were-deer, quite pretty in both her forms. "When you come of age, each of you will discover your own alternate form," she explained. "No one knows ahead of time what it may be, and we don't know what determines it. So we try to educate you about all types of animals, large and small, so that when it happens you will at least know something about your kind. Questions?"

Wetzel had one. "What about were-animals? How are they different from us?" Because he had encountered the were-mice, even if he never spoke of them.

"That is an excellent question, Wetzel," Weava said. Her spot favor made him feel good. "The were ability extends widely, and many animals do have it too. But they are more limited. For example, were-mice can transform to snakes, nothing else. Humans can transform into virtually any kind of animal, and retain human intelligence in those other forms."

"What do snakes transform to?" a girl asked.

"Birds. And birds transform to other reptiles."

It was an interesting lesson. Wetzel, like the other children, wondered what his alternate form would be. A tiger? An eagle? A crocodile? He hoped it wouldn't be a mouse.

Part of education turned out to be the arts. The children were encouraged to draw, paint, sculpt, sing, dance, or act. Different ones had different talents. Wetzel's turned out to be drama: he could play a role convincingly, once he learned it. He enjoyed being in plays.

Two years later another boy developed precocious telepathy. Wetzel could tell, because the child was reveling in it, peeking into girls' minds to see their secrets, trying to see what they saw in the mirror when they undressed and washed. He discovered that he could make them focus on such things when he spoke of them: "What's in your panties?" They told him to go wash out his mouth with soap, but their minds showed their naked bodies. He also cheated at guessing games by reading the answers in the other minds.

It was becoming clear to Wetzel why the adults did not want children to have telepathy. It was too easy to abuse, when most lacked it. Wetzel had not abused it, mainly because he had been too busy hiding it.

Within a day that boy was gone. No one spoke of him thereafter.

They grew and learned, until it seemed there was nothing more to learn. But there was, as they were drilled in discipline. They had to fathom right and wrong, and do what was right, regardless of their preferences. It was one big bore, but they had no choice. No one protested, because no one wanted to disappear.

At last their group reached the magic age of eighteen, the official age of maturity. They knew there would be drastic changes, because they were about to become adults. Already their bodies were developing, especially the girls, who formed breasts and wider hips.

Now they were addressed in a special class, apart from the younger ones. "Soon you will be achieving the art of telepathy," Weava the were-deer said. "It normally happens at the time of puberty. Then a year or so after puberty comes your first transformation. That is when you will discover your alternate form."

This was interesting, though familiar. It got more so.

"You, the class of you, have been suppressed, so that none of these changes occurs prematurely. Now that suppression has been released, and you will be discovering the formidable assets and liabilities of the adult state. This month we will guide you to the realization of your inherent telepathic ability."

It was true. Guided by the teacher, they smoothed out their minds and let the awareness come. It was familiar to Wetzel, but novel for the others. He played along, of course. It was surprising how readily the others picked up on it. It was a natural ability, so they were not learning it so much as discovering it, now that the suppression was gone. In a way it was like finding a new house and entering it for the first time. Soon the wonder faded, but the constant awareness of other minds did not. It was a new dimension of experience.

Then came the second aspect of the adult triad. "At this time you will be initiated into sexual expression," Weava announced. "We will now demonstrate exactly what happens during sex."

Could that be true? Wetzel was as bemused as the others in the class. How could they suddenly demonstrate what had been so carefully hidden before, throughout?

They did. An adult man and an adult woman stripped to show their full nude bodies. They stroked each other and the man's penis got stiff. "The purpose of the man's erection is to make it feasible for him to penetrate the woman and ejaculate his semen into her body," the teacher continued. "Left to nature, this could impregnate her, and she would in due course bear a baby. However, all of you have been dosed in your food with contraceptive agents that will prevent conception. We do not want any girl conceiving until her adult transformation is complete, and she understands the full ramifications of the act. For these few months your only purpose in having sex is to enjoy it and learn how to do it properly. Only then will you have the background to make mature decisions about life relationships."

The students exchanged glances. This was amazing! Suddenly everything that had been withheld from them was being explained and encouraged. Including the mystery of why they had had little or no interest in sex before, merely curiosity about what was hidden. That, like the telepathy, had been suppressed.

"First the physical component," Weava continued as if unaware of the phenomenal impact this lesson was having on the students. The girls were blushing, and every boy had an erection, one of the embarrassing phenomena of sexual maturity. The teacher seemed not to notice. This was, it seemed, routine for her.

The demonstrators proceeded to perform the act, each stage described by the teacher. The woman lay on the bed while the man mounted her, set his hard penis at her cleft, and slowly pushed it into her body. Then he withdrew it part way, and thrust deeper. After several times he grunted with fulfillment and relaxed. When he got off the woman his penis was going limp, and dripping. He had, as Weava described, ejaculated into her vagina.

The students watched it all, fascinated and repelled. They were supposed to learn how to do this? Erections were one thing, but doing *that* with them?

"There are many variations," the teacher said, "but this is the essence. We will in the next few days acquaint you with those variations of position, and with the types of manual and oral sexual expression. But today you must learn the mental side of it. Because, you see, both partners are telepathic. They can and do feel each other's climaxes. This lends a phenomenal extra dimension to the experience. You need to be thoroughly familiar with this aspect before you first have sex."

"But the demonstrators just did it," a girl protested. "We didn't feel any—any climax."

"That aspect was suppressed," Weava explained. "So as not to distract you from the observation of the mechanics. The next demonstration will be complete with the experience of the orgasm."

She smiled. "You will not forget that."

Indeed, another couple demonstrated, and this time the entire class experienced the man's orgasm. It certainly would have been a distraction.

"The man gets the—the feeling," a boy said. "Not the woman?"

"Not as readily," the teacher said. "But she can, especially when the man is attentive to her needs and responses. Both parties can share that too. That will be demonstrated another day."

Weava went on to explain that in other cultures women were sometimes raped. That was when the man was so eager for sex that he forced it on an unwilling woman. "But in our culture, rape is impossible." And she explained why: if the woman did not want sex, her mental aversion spread to the man and he lost his erection and thus his ability to perform penetration. In fact she could so focus her thoughts as to make him lose it even if she was not averse to it. "The man has physical control, but the woman has mental control," the teacher explained. "Of the two, the latter is more powerful. No girl will graduate from this class until she demonstrates the power to render a man impotent."

Then she smiled. "This, too, we will now demonstrate. A volunteer, please." She glanced at Wetzel. "You."

He was floored. "Me?"

"Step to the front of the class and strip off your clothing."

He was appalled. "But—but I have a—"

"Precisely." With her telepathy Weava knew his state. She had been aware of the reactions of the boys and girls throughout. "Now."

He had to obey. In that moment he realized that she knew about his own premature telepathy. That was why she had chosen him. The others were still uncertain in their mind readings, but he knew how from long experience. In moments he was naked before the class, his erection manifest.

"Like this," the teacher said, approaching him. She was actually an attractive adult; several boys had had crushes on her before this. Wetzel might have, but had quickly buried the feeling in the emotional storm cellar of his haunted house. What was she going to do with him? He half dreaded, half relished the thought. To put his stiff member into a woman like her . . .

Weava looked at him.

Something changed in his mind. Not only did he lose interest in sex, he detested the very thought of it. His erection faded. His penis descended and shrank.

There was a titter in the class. His performance was humiliating. The one thing worse than having his erection exposed in public was losing it in public. Without sex.

"Every girl will have this ability," the teacher said. She clapped her hands. "Class dismissed."

Chaos erupted as the students compared notes and impressions. Wetzel was left standing in his shame.

Weava turned to him. "I selected you because I fathomed your telepathy, Wetzel," she said. "You have had it for some time, but since you did not abuse it, we let you be. That makes you vulnerable to this suppression. Without sufficient telepathy you would not have been able to read my suppressive thought. It was not my purpose to embarrass you, though of course I did. I had to make it quite clear to all of you what the girls will be learning. Now I will make it worth your while, knowing that you like me. Dress and come to my house."

What could he do? He dressed and meekly followed her.

She led him to her house and brought him inside. "Now you may have your first tangible heterosexual experience. This time I will not suppress your erection." She undressed, had him undress, and joined him on the bed. His erection was back, as hard as before. "Show me how well you learned today's lessen."

And in minutes he did. Guided by her quiet words, he got on her and in her. He did not climax as fast as the demonstrator man had, but after many thrusts, encouraged by the teacher, he succeeded getting his first orgasm. It was enhanced by his realization that she could have aborted it at any time, but had not. Did she actually like him back, maybe a little?

She kissed him as he concluded. "Was it worth it?"

"Oh, yes!" he gasped.

"I always liked you, Wetzel," she said, answering his thought. "You're smart, you behave well, and there's something appealing about you. In due course you will practice sex with the girls of other villages, as they mature. In the interim, I will be at your service." She smiled again. "And yes, you may talk about this incident, and I will confirm it. You have technically become a man."

His suppressed crush on her burgeoned. Fully aware, she held him and kissed him again before dismissing him.

So it was. He did talk about it; indeed he could not avoid it, because others had seen the teacher take him to her house, and asked him. He had become the teacher's pet, a mark of favor. The adults, of course, already knew. He suspected they had read his mind as he penetrated her, getting a vicarious first experience. Weava had known exactly what she was doing. At any rate, his embarrassment had been wholly erased. He was now the envy of the other boys.

The girls were drilled in the suppressive technique, while the boys were instructed in sexual manners. Virginity, they were assured, was unimportant; what counted was the mutuality of the experience. If a girl foiled a boy's erection, he was still at liberty to attempt to persuade her to allow the completion of the act. Success was its own reward. The students were not sexually or romantically interested in each other; they had associated too closely, too long. But the class was taken to visit the next village, whose teens had been similarly educated, and soon boys and girls were paring off to practice. The couples were assigned by the teachers; it was not romantic.

"Here is the rule," Weava said. "You will all strip nude. Each boy will attempt to penetrate his ad-hoc girlfriend. She will attempt to foil him, not physically, but by mentally stunting his erection. If she does not succeed, she will accommodate him gracefully. If she does, he will compliment her on her proficiency."

Wetzel's partner was Weena. She was a sultry brunette, and her breasts were not large but firm and well defined; she was more woman than girl. "Try it, big boy," she murmured. "I'll even let you take hold of me first."

She had confidence. Was it warranted? He put his arms about her, his member rampant.

And stood there as it sank into oblivion. Damn!

She smiled, picking up his thought.

"Congratulations," he said, uncertain whether he was frustrated or relieved.

Weena laughed. "You're a good sport. Now I'll let you do it for real, if you like."

"No, you won. I got to do it only if you couldn't stop me."

"Or if you could then persuade me. You can if you try."

But he was confused, embarrassed, and uncertain. "No."

She shrugged, hardly concerned. "Suit yourself."

Later he wondered why he had demurred, after being so eager for it before. And realized it was because of Weava. He knew she would give him sex, and he really didn't want it with anyone else.

As it turned out, none of the boys succeeded; all the girls of both villages had learned the melting thought. But it was an excellent demonstration of its effectiveness. Most of the girls had then relented and let the boys have it. As the teacher had said, virginity was nothing; sex was fun to do, because the girls could read the climatic passions of the boys, thus also experiencing them. With telepathy there was no such thing as one-sided sex; if one person got an orgasm, both did.

Another week they went to a third village for more practice. And there Wetzel was astonished.

His assigned partner was a svelte blonde with corkscrew curls. She seemed oddly familiar. "Don't you recognize me?" she inquired coyly.

"Willa!" His childhood acquaintance had matured into an impressive young woman.

"Hello, Wetzel," she said.

"But—but I thought you—"

"You were supposed to," she said. "I was merely moved to a special camp for precocious telepaths. As it turned out, I was physically precocious too." She half turned, inhaling, showing off her full breasts and tiny waist. She was certainly more mature physically than the other girls. "I asked to join you here, and they let me, though I have long since demonstrated my ability to foil sex. Not that I ever really wanted to. Let's get more private."

"But this is a class!" He was still stunned by the discovery that she was not only alive, but completely healthy.

Willa raised one hand in a signal. Her teacher nodded.

"This way," she said, leading him to a house.

Inside, they talked, catching up on the years they had been apart. "I hated letting you think I was dead," she said. "But I was forbidden to contact you. The message that girls *don't* play show-me with boys had to be made brutally clear."

"That was the reason? I thought the telepathy—"

"Telepathy was the real reason," she agreed. "The show-me was the fake reason. They don't want precocious telepaths among the children, and they don't want it known how many there are. So they sequester them. You were lucky they didn't sequester you."

"I thought I was hiding it."

"You did, for some time. They were impressed. So they let you be as long as you behaved, and you did behave. But now you can let go."

The teacher had told him the same thing. "That's nice." But his lifelong caution remained, and he did not tell her about the mental storm shelter. He did not know at what point they had caught on to his telepathy; it might be fairly recent.

"I always liked you," she said. "As I guess I made clear in the haunted house. That's why I wanted to play the game of show-me with you."

"And we never quite did it," he said ruefully.

"We'll do it now." She started removing her clothing.

Now his caution became intense. Why was she coming on to him like this? He quickly buried the thought. "No need. I have already seen it."

"We'll do more than see. I'll pretend I can't foil your erection." She smiled knowingly. "In fact, I'll show you how a girl can do the opposite. It's really the same ability, reversed. I can make it so hard you just have to use it."

"You can do that?"

"You doubt?" And suddenly he had an almost painfully stiff erection, and the desire to use it, exactly as she had said. It did make sense that control went both ways. It wasn't thought projection so much as his inability *not* to read the insidiously suggestive thought she made.

And yet he hardly knew her, really, which meant she hardly

knew him. They were no longer children. She was attractive, oh yes, but he did not trust this at all. He picked up a fleetingly unguarded thought in her mind. "Don't you have a boyfriend?"

"Dung!" she swore. "You caught on."

So she did have a boyfriend. Her interest in Wetzel had to be something else. "Why are you trying to seduce me?"

"Damn, I was too obvious. Now I've blown it." She sighed. "Okay, you won the game, and I have to submit gracefully, even if it's not the way I figured. You're too damn smart. You're right: they want to know something about you, and they can't fathom it, so they sent me to weasel it out of you."

"Weasel what?"

"How you're hiding. They know you've been snooping on the other children for years, you had to have been, because their minds were unguarded and open to you. But there's no sign of it in your thoughts. You're just an ordinary innocent boy. How do you do it? That's what they want to know, and they know you won't tell them voluntarily."

So he *had* succeeded in hiding in the storm shelter. That was gratifying to confirm. If it was true.

Wetzel shook his head. "I wish you had come to me of your own accord, Willa," he said. "Then I would have trusted you."

"I wish I had too. I've blown it, but that's the least of it. I really do like you, Wetzel, always did. There's something about you. But I tried to betray you, and you don't deserve it. I know myself now to be dishonest, and I hate it." She met his gaze, and he saw that her eyes were bright with tears. "I won't bother you any more. I wish you well in life, Wetzel. I doubt that we will meet again."

It might be a ploy, but he was moved. "What happens to you if you fail?"

"At least I can leave you with the truth. That boyfriend—I love him, but he is using me. For this. Failure means I'll lose him."

Almost, he relented. "Willa—"

"Hold your course, Wetzel. I'm lost, in this respect, but you aren't. Fare well." And she held out her hand.

He shook it, appreciating the honesty of their parting. Had she kissed him she might have won him, and she knew it. Then they walked back to the class, and separated.

CHAPTER 2: VIRGIN

"That's too bad," Weava said sympathetically after they had sex. She had picked it up from his turbulent thoughts, and given him what he might have had with Willa, defusing that frustration to an extent. "Otherwise you might have made it with her. She's a good girl, but was put in a situation."

"I understand," Wetzel said. "She did what she had to do. But still it hurts." Then he had an alarming thought.

"No," Weava said immediately. "I was not party to that ploy. I thought she merely wanted to surprise you with her identity, and perhaps leave her scheming boyfriend for you. I know you have secrets; I believe you are entitled to them. Telepathy magnifies the sexual experience, yet there is one aspect it diminishes: mystery. Some of the allure is lost when the partners have no secrets from each other. That is one reason I refused to interrogate you about this, so they evidently sought elsewhere."

That had not occurred to him. "I intrigue you because I have secrets?"

"You do, Wetzel. Our sexual relationship is temporary, until you discover your were-form and find romance, but it's fun. You will make some girl a fine partner."

He liked her tolerance and her support. "That partner can't be you?"

"I am seventeen years older than you, almost twice your age. You would find that tiring in time. But more important, I am dedicated to my profession. I will never stop teaching. You are surely destined for more dramatic things. You are a creature of adventure, externally and internally. I refuse to tie you down to a relative dullard like me, whatever the appeal of the moment."

Wetzel wanted to protest, but realized she was correct. She had also found a very nice way to let him know she wasn't interested in a long-term romance with him.

"And you are uncommonly perceptive and rational," she added, smiling.

He had to laugh. "And you are expert in finessing awkward expectations."

"I'm a teacher. It comes with the territory." Then she kissed him, and everything was fine.

"You are," he agreed. Maybe if he were really lucky he would find a girl who would become a woman like her.

"And you have a rare touch with a compliment," she said.

He felt a surge of emotion. "Let me love you, this moment."

"I thought you'd never ask." They had just had sex, but she used her power to enhance his virility so that he could do it again. This was a pleasant response, but still a diversion from his real wish to love her romantically. She was still handling him, interpreting his emotion conveniently, and making him like it without hurting his feelings. Sex was easy for her to give, rather than love.

"But I could love you, if I let myself," she murmured as they finished. "I always liked you, and had to rule myself sternly not to favor you in class. You are worthy, Wetzel."

"Thank you." What else could he say? Through all the years he had never realized that she favored him, despite his mind reading ability. He had known better than to even try reading hers, sure she would recognize the feather touch.

"You are appealing to women," she continued. "Whether they are immature or adult. This helped you in drama; the girls liked to play opposite you."

"I thought they just liked dressing up and acting."

"That, too."

In the following year not only did the class become fully proficient in sexual expression, they started discovering their alternate forms. Each day Weava conducted a group session wherein they all blanked their minds and made themselves receptive to whatever might come. At first it seemed like a pointless exercise, but then a girl abruptly made an exclamation and transformed to a songbird. She had found her form.

Thereafter others found theirs, becoming cats, horses, hawks, crocodiles, and bears. There seemed to be no predictable pattern; the changes were random. Until only one was left: Wetzel.

"You have a form," Weava assured him. "Everyone does. You merely have to discover it."

"But where is it? Why am I so slow?"

She considered. "Sometimes a person doesn't like his other form, so refuses to use it."

"Like the boy who became a skunk," Wetzel agreed. "He wasn't pleased."

"Yet it's worthy. All forms are worthy. A were-skunk can patrol silently at night, guarding premises, and can really stop an intruder."

"I don't want to be a skunk."

"Whatever you are, it will be worthy," she said. "There is that in you that is very special. It merely takes time to manifest."

"You are handling me again, preparing me for disappointment."

"Stop that!" she flared. Amazed, he realized she was angry; the heat of it beat at his mind. He had never seen her even annoyed before. "I am telling you the truth. You are special, and your alternate form will be special. I know it."

"I apologize," he said quickly, awed by her rare emotion. "But how do you know?"

"We can't predict the exact forms, but sometimes we can get a general notion. Something is looming in you, something truly remarkable, unlike any our village has seen before. It will amaze everyone. We have to ensure that it emerges properly, and that you are ready for it, because there could be liabilities along with its power. So that you don't—" She broke off.

"Don't what?"

She frowned, then answered. "Don't reject it."

"Why would I do that?"

"The liability might seem to make it not worthwhile for you. This is too important to allow rejection."

"*That's* why you're with me! To be sure I don't mess it up!"

Now he saw tears in her eyes, just as he had with Willa. "I'm so sorry, Wetzel. It is true."

He schooled himself to be rational. She had never promised him a long association, only a temporary one. That was unchanged. Only her reason was different. "Damn."

"You have a right to be angry. Everything I have told you is true. I just did not tell you the whole of it. You are worthy, I do like you, it is for the moment, but I would have had to be with you regardless. This can not be left to chance."

Had he handled himself better with Willa, he might have won her. Instead he had thrown her away on a technicality, angry because she was assigned to interrogate him. It was pointless to do the same with Weava. "Please, if it's so important but I might mess it up, I want you to be on my side."

"I will help you in whatever way I can."

"That's evasion. I want you as my friend. I need to know I can trust your advice, whatever it may be."

"I *am* your friend."

"You're my teacher and my lover. That's not the same."

"*And* your friend. Read my mind."

He did. Her thoughts and emotions were mixed, but she truly wanted what was best for him. She always had. She did not love him, but intended to do right by him.

"I apologize for doubting you."

"No need. You are right to be skeptical. No one likes to be used."

"How am I being used?"

"If your were-form turns out to be valuable to the village, you will be required to remain here, regardless of your preference."

"Why would I want to leave?"

"I don't know, but there are indications you will not be satisfied here. So your freedom may be at stake."

He did not like the sound of this, buttressed by her genuine concern. "What is your advice, as a friend?"

She leaned forward and whispered urgently. "Depart. Leave the village. Now, before you transform. Only in this manner can you be assured of your freedom."

"But then I would have to leave all my friends. And you. For a nebulous speculation that I may want to in the future. Does this make sense?"

"Yes, Wetzel, it does. We are dealing with probabilities, and they indicate that you could become a virtual prisoner here. That you could become unhappy. Even if I remained your lover, which I may have to do."

His own emotions were becoming chaotic. "This would bother you?"

"Yes, because I want your sexual interest because you have it naturally, as now, rather than because you have no alternative, as may become the case. Wetzel, I want you to realize your full potential in every manner, and I fear you can not achieve that here."

"You said you could love me if you allowed it. Would you allow it?"

"Yes. But I think that would not be enough. I am not your perfect mate now, and I will be less so as time passes. Especially once you achieve transformation. You thought I was being polite, but it is true: I would tie you down. I am not in your league for potential. I am not worthy of you."

"Weava!" he cried, pained.

"It is the truth."

And her mind, completely open to him, echoed that. She truly believed that he was destined for greatness, and that she would only be in the way.

"I can't do it," he said. "This village has been everything to me. And you—I can't leave you. Not until you tell me it's over."

"Trust me," she said. "You must go."

"I can't."

She sighed. "If you should change your mind, don't consult with me or anyone. Just go without notice. That may be your best chance."

That much he could promise, knowing he was unlikely to change his mind. "Agreed."

"Let's not discuss this further. You need to keep it out of your thoughts."

"I can do that."

She smiled. "Yes you can. Do not tell me your secret. You may need it."

Love for her overwhelmed him. "I'll tell you."

"No!" Then, rather than debate the matter, she sent him the potency thought. Soon they were having sex a third time. By the time it was done he realized that she was surely right, and that he needed to keep his secret, even from her. He buried their dialogue in the storm shelter.

But why did she think he would want to leave the village and her, when no harm threatened him?

Time passed, and nothing happened. Weava encouraged him to go out and have liaisons with the girls of neighboring villages, but he demurred. He knew she was trying to get him out of the local village, so that he could more readily depart it forever. But he needed neither the girls nor departure, as long as he had Weava. He was in temporary love.

And realized one day when he visited the storm shelter, that the powers that existed in the village had known he wouldn't leave Weava, regardless what she told him. He was thoroughly smitten. So she had been free to tell him the truth as she saw it. He was already committed to the village. She bound him here despite wanting to free him. It was an irony she surely understood and was pained by.

He tried to make himself useful despite his indeterminate status as an incomplete person. Weava qualified him as an assistant teacher and demonstrator. He explained to the class following his own class how telepathy worked.

"Every brain constantly radiates thoughts," he said. "They zip outward like little arrows until at last they lose coherence and are lost in the welter of the radiations of other people. It is like a lamp whose light becomes dim with distance. Only at close range, when the thoughts are dense and strong, are they really intelligible to anyone else.

"We do not send thoughts to specific targets, such as our friends; we merely send them out evenly in all directions. But when two heads come together, their radiations can interact. Normally they just pass through each other without touching. But when one person focuses on another, there can be a tangible interaction. His thoughts collide with those of the other person, like two boys running into each other, and the radiation from that collision then goes out. Some of those reflected thoughts return to that person's mind, and he knows what the other is thinking. It is only a tiny random sample, one part in a hundred or a thousand, but if the thoughts are massed on something like chocolate cake, that's enough to do it." He smiled, as thoughts of chocolate cake suffused the classroom. "Some of that collision radiation returns to the person being snooped on, and he feels a feather-light mental touch. We will teach all of you to become sensitive to that touch, so you will always know when a mind is reading yours." He looked at a girl. "I am focusing on your mind now, intercepting your thoughts. Can you feel the touch?"

"Yes," she said, surprised. "I—I have been feeling them all along, from all around. I just didn't realize what they were."

"You are pretty. That's why the boys want to get into you, so to speak." There was more embarrassed laughter, but the point had been made.

"This has repercussions," he continued. "Especially if the thoughts are of sex." Now sex suffused the room, as the students responded; they could not help it, being novices at telepathy. "This is the secret of the rape preventive. A girl does not send the suppression to the boy; she merely puts it strongly in her mind, and when he reads her mind he gets it. He can if he chooses prevent being turned off; all he has to do is respect her privacy and stay out of her mind." Now there was embarrassed laughter. "And of course he can do it too, not that he wants to. Instead he prefers to let thoughts of passionate sex prevail, and if she reads his mind that passion becomes hers and she wants it as much as he does. So it behooves her, too, to respect his privacy, if she does not want to have sex with him. Since reading minds is a deliberate conscious act, it is easy enough to respect privacy." Privacy was perhaps the most vital concept following the onset of telepathy. That was why students were carefully monitored and guided throughout their maturation.

"You make a good teacher," Weava said approvingly after the class.

"I learned from a good teacher." Yet he was unsatisfied.

What was his were-form? Why was it so late in manifesting? How important could it be? And what was its liability, that might make him want to flee?

"Please," he said to Weava one day. "I am consumed by curiosity. What are my were-prospects?"

This she could answer. "We suspect that though most folk are limited to ordinary were-forms, such as mammals, birds, reptiles or even insects, you may go beyond."

"Beyond? What else is there?"

"Fantasy creatures."

"You mean things that don't exist? Ogres, dragons, ghosts?"

"Yes. Or creatures with special magic powers."

"Magic is illusion. I mean, there is no such thing."

"Not in our frame," she agreed.

"There are other frames? You never taught us this in class."

"I was not allowed to. The authorities feel it would be disruptive. But other frames do exist. Sometimes we are visited by them. This is not common knowledge."

"I'll say! How could I become a fantasy creature I know nothing about?"

"What you become does not depend on what you know. We teach you all the normal creatures so you will have basis to relate when you become one of them. So you will not be unduly confused. Now perhaps you should study fantasy creatures, just in case."

"When I was small, I feared ghosts," he said. "Willa pooh-poohed that, and I think she was correct. I have not believed in them since."

"Believe in them now," she said. "You may become one."

"A ghost? They are intangible."

"Or a similar spook that is tangible. When you enter the supernatural, there is no limit."

"I find it hard to believe you are saying this. You have always been my most sensible teacher."

She smiled. "I remain sensible. I am trying to prepare you for what may happen. When the ordinary no longer applies, the extraordinary comes into play."

He shook his head, bemused. "That would explain why they would want to keep me here. A real live dragon would be a considerable tourist draw."

She did not laugh. "It would. Fun for the tourists. Not for the dragon."

But he simply couldn't credit it.

Meanwhile he was not considered fully adult until he achieved his were-form, so could not assume the prerogatives of citizenship. He was in limbo, in between, physically mature but incomplete. He was marking time.

A year passed, during which he learned all about fantasy animals and the many manners of sex. Weava was an excellent teacher in both. He performed routine village chores, as was a citizen's duty; others allowed this, anticipating his eventual transition. Several classmates found partners and moved to other villages, while several new men moved in to marry local girls. There was no set rule, but normally women did remain home while men traveled. Wetzel did not want to admit it, but he was becoming bored with the local village life. Even though he loved his continuing affair with Weava, and liked assisting her in the classes she taught, especially drama, the prospect of adventure elsewhere was appealing more strongly.

Unless Weava would agree to marry him and bear his children. That might be all the adventure he needed. He did want to be a family man, at least after sowing his wild oats. But she would not. She had allowed herself to love him, but she refused to bind him. She would be his lover, not his wife.

Then, when he least expected it, it happened. He was walking through the nearby woods on the way to a fruit orchard when he abruptly transformed. Into a horse. A pure white stallion.

Except that there was a long spiraling horn projecting from his equine forehead. It took him moments to make sense of this anomaly. Then it connected.

He was not a horse, but a unicorn. A were-unicorn.

He quickly reverted to his normal form, and discovered that he had lost his clothing. His shirt and pants had burst asunder when he transformed, and were now rags.

Well, it hardly mattered. He tied on the tattered pants and ran back to the village to tell Weava.

"You transformed!" she exclaimed, reading his mind.

"To a unicorn," he agreed, kissing her.

"Darn."

"But you were right. I'm a fantasy animal."

"The liability," she said carefully. "Don't you know what it is?"

Now he remembered. "The unicorn's horn is magical. It can penetrate any armor in combat. It can purify water merely by being dipped in it. It can cure illness and heal wounds, by touch. So people try to kill unicorns for their horns."

"That too."

"What else?" he asked, slightly nettled.

"Do you still want to marry me?"

"Well, of course I do." Then he paused, startled. "No I don't."

"Why not?"

"Because—because you're not a virgin."

"True. You and I have had sex four hundred times."

"This is ridiculous," he protested, wondering peripherally whether she had kept count. As a teacher, she tended to be precise. "You're a wonderful woman, and I love you, and—" He paused again, chagrined. "I no longer love you."

"I have not changed."

"You have not," he agreed. "You are as wonderful as ever, and I know it. But I have. I am no longer capable of truly loving a non-virgin."

"And that is the significant liability of the unicorn," she said. "He is emotionally vulnerable to virgins. A virgin can make you do anything. Until you have your way with her."

Wetzel worked it out. "I can have sex, but I can't marry, because after sex her virginity is gone. It's not rational, but that is now my fickle nature." He considered the problem. "But I believe I can have sex with a non-virgin. You remain sexually appealing to me."

"Sex without love," she agreed. "Or love without sex. These are now your choices."

"And it will be the same wherever I might go. Damn!"

She sighed. "I gave you sex without love, originally. Now you can return the favor by giving it to me."

"Why should I treat you that way?"

"Because you do still like sex, and you are magically appealing. You will have all the women you want, who will be fascinated by your mere presence, whichever form you use. Beginning with me."

"You want sex with me, knowing that I have lost my love for you?"

"Yes. I know you will not stay with me now, so I want it while I can get it."

"Weava, this is unkind. I don't want to treat you like that."

"Please. The urge is very strong."

What could he do? "As you wish."

"This way," she said, and transformed to her deer form.

Startled, he considered. The unicorn and the deer were different species. But they were not really different; they were alternate forms of two people who had already had sex many times. So it was not miscegenation. She wanted to be the first to do it with him in his new form. How could he deny her that?

He tried to mount her from behind, but he was far larger as a unicorn than she was as a deer, and it simply wasn't feasible. She realized it too, and changed back. He rejoined her in human form, and they assumed the animal position, emulating what they could not actually do. That turned out to be enough. While it was good for him, physically, he knew from her mind that it was phenomenal for her. There was indeed something about a unicorn, whatever the form of the moment.

She kissed him. "Be warned," she said as they relaxed. "I am not the only older woman in the village who will crave your attention. Any you get near to, single or married, will do her best to get you quickly into her. Your young classmates too; they will no longer care that they grew up with you. It's a man's dream: every woman eager."

"But I don't want to mess with them! Few are pretty, and none of them are virgins." Then he shook his head. "What a callow rake I have become. You're right: I should leave before the jealous men burn me at the stake."

"I fear you should, though you will not find satisfaction elsewhere. Oh Wetzel, I wish you had achieved some other form!"

"So do I. I'll go now, to spare you more pain you don't deserve."

"Do that," she said tearfully.

Wetzel packed his few belongings in a backpack, including several shirts and pairs of pants, and walked to the edge of the village. And stopped.

A row of armed men barred his way. The villagers had learned of his transformation, which could hardly have been concealed considering the telepathy, and were acting to confine him to the village. He knew why: as a unicorn he could do their water supply much good, and he could facilitate all manner of recoveries and cures. He had become a valuable village asset.

Weava's prior warning had been apt. He should have left the village while he could. Now he would either have to fight his way out, or accept his situation.

He did not want to hurt anyone, even if he could then heal them. Wordlessly he turned about and walked back into the village.

"I feared that," Weava said, kissing him. "We shall have to barricade my house, at least until the villagers get organized to protect it."

Because if the men were already out, so were the women. A number of them stood in sight, and when Wetzel glanced at them, they opened their shirts invitingly. There was no subtlety, physically or mentally. They wanted raw sex.

"He is mine," Weava announced, and shut them out. Then inside: "But you are not mine. I am only shielding you to the extent I can. That won't be effective long."

"Not long," he agreed. "Oh Weava, what can we do?"

"We must be practical. If any woman gets inside the house, don't argue with her. Screw her, literally. Then she'll go and we can block off the entry she found, to prevent others from using it."

"But you—how can you encourage me to do that?"

"I have discovered that the sex we had satisfies me, at least for now. It may be several hours before your presence overwhelms me again. So I am being practical. We must try to keep the women at bay until we figure out how to get you out of here."

"I should have heeded your advice, before."

"You should have," she agreed. "Yet I can't say I'm entirely sorry you didn't. Once I made the mistake of letting myself love you, I wanted your frequent embrace."

"You should have remained emotionally aloof," he agreed sadly.

"Now I know that it was the precursor to your unicorn state that made you so appealing. It was just too easy to fall. I did know better. Now I will pay."

"Weava," he said, pained.

She shrugged. "Hardly my first mistake, and surely not my last. I will handle it."

"When I escape, come with me!"

"You don't even love me!" she flared. "The point is you must get away by yourself, and somewhere, somehow, find your destiny. If you want my company, you will have to return here."

She was correct. "But of course they won't let me go."

"You can escape," she said persuasively. "Simply seduce the chief's wife into sneaking you out. She knows how."

He shook his head. "Not that way. I must depart honestly or not at all. You taught me integrity."

"Unfortunately I did. But this is a dishonest situation. They have no right to hold you here."

"That does not justify dishonesty on my part. You taught me that too."

She sighed. "I taught you too well. Very well, for now. We must deal with the hand we have been dealt. You will remain and service the local women as they require. The challenge will be the virgins."

"I don't want to service anyone!"

"Be rational. The married women will demand it, and their husbands will let them."

"Why should they do that?"

"You have never lived with a woman who is determined to have her way."

He laughed. "Only you."

"Touché. Believe me, the husbands will allow it, because the wives will either divorce them or make them wish they were divorced unless they accede. This isn't infidelity; you're a unicorn! They will probably set up a schedule. You will accede because you will have no choice. Husbands, too, can be brutally persuasive. But as I said, the challenge will be the virgins. They are the only ones you will want, and also the only ones not interested in you. You will have to learn the art of courtship."

"But any virgin I seduce I will lose interest in."

"Exactly. Then a man can marry her knowing that she will thereafter be true to him, since you won't touch her again."

Wetzel had a problem with this. "If married women want me, why wouldn't ex-virgins?"

"Oh, they would. But they would be women loved and scorned. It will take them some time to get over that."

"You understand this better than I do."

"I do," she agreed. "It comes with being of the feminine persuasion myself. I suggest that you follow my advice now. This will enable us to live in this village without undue strife."

"I can stay with you?"

"Yes, if you want to."

Wetzel spoke carefully, clarifying his emotions as he did. "I can't say I love you now, though I wish I could. But I know you for the excellent person you are, and I trust you. You are my friend. I like your company. I want to remain with you. I will give you sex any time you wish it. Is this a fair compromise?"

"Yes, Wetzel. Give me sex now." Her need was burgeoning, now that some time had passed; he felt it coming at him, though she was not using the stimulus thought on him. She simply couldn't help her passion in his presence.

He embraced her and got to it, making sure she got her climax. He shared that, and it was good. Then they slept.

The following days played out as Weava had predicted. Wetzel bedded one wife a day, catering to her so that she was fully satisfied. Meanwhile he learned the seductive art from Weava and practiced it on one virgin at a time. It was indeed a challenge, but with persistence and increasing skill he did manage to seduce each village virgin. These were by far his most satisfying liaisons, but each ended the moment he succeeded. Virginity was of the mind as much as of the body; once a woman had sex she was changed, her original naïveté gone. It was that emotional freshness that he craved. He left behind a series of angry young women, even though the rules of this game had been clear from the outset. Each foolishly hoped to be the exception.

He also transformed and used his horn to guarantee the purity of the village water supply, to heal wounds, and cure ailments. When a rogue bear attacked the village, Wetzel speared it with his horn and left it dead. He did have formidable physical and magical powers, and was certainly paying his way. In fact he could have run the gantlet of men barring his departure, killed them, and escaped. But he was determined to leave peacefully or not at all. It was his compromise with his situation. He knew it and they knew it, because of the telepathy. He did not bother to hide it; why should he?

He could have been happy this way, as he had everything a normal man might want: sustenance and plenty of sex. Except for the one thing: he could not love a non-virgin, and he could not keep a virgin. It was the paradox of his unicorn identity. If there was a resolution, it was not here. He doubted it was anywhere, because it was inherent in his nature, but at least he could dream that somewhere in the universe there was an answer. A virgin he could both love and keep.

"I wish I could be that virgin," Weava said sadly.

"I wish so too. You are the perfect woman. I know it. But I just can't—"

"I understand," she said. And she did. That was part of her tragedy.

Then he spied the trail. It came up to Weava's house and terminated. It led through the village without touching it, winding into an unknown realm. He tried to fathom it via telepathy, but found only nonsense: *Beetle Juice*. He followed it briefly, then, nervous, returned to the house.

"What is it?" he asked Weava. She was able to see the trail only when he held her hand and faced it.

"That is your legitimate escape," she answered. "I know of it only through legend, but it seems it is true. It is an aspect of an entity known as the Amoeba that spans all our universe and all time and all alternate universes. Few, very few, are ever offered the privilege of joining it. This is your destiny, Wetzel. You must take that trail."

"Come with me!"

"I can not."

"Try." He held her hand and led her onto the trail. They walked a short distance into it, and the village faded. "See?" he said, letting her hand go.

She vanished.

Alarmed, he ran back off the trail. There she was, standing in the street. "When you let go, I reverted to my own frame. This is for you alone."

He fought the notion, but during the night, between frenzied bouts of sex, she persuaded him. He would take the trail, leaving her and the village behind. It represented his peaceful compromise. His chance to discover his greater destiny. His search for the Virgin. This persuasion was Weava's final gift to him.

But he could not do it without giving her an equivalent gift. He would share his secret with her.

"But you must not," she protested. "I never asked you to do that."

"It is my virginity," he agreed. "My own personal privacy. I want you to have it to remember me by. You are the one person who deserves it. You don't have to share it; it can be your secret too."

"I can not deny that the idea of learning it fascinates me," she said. "But I think I would prefer to have you keep it. That's safer."

"If I am gone, and you keep it, it will remain secret. It is my ultimate trust in you."

She could not demur further. He became the teacher, guiding her to his most secret place, the storm shelter, and showing her the precious secrets stored there.

"Oh, it's wonderful!" she exclaimed as she looked around, clapping her hands like a little girl.

And the telepathy was so close and intense that they were both in the haunted cellar, seeing each other there.

"You can even take off your clothes and show me your secret place, if you want to," he said smiling. "You are my first and only visitor. My virgin of the moment."

"I want to. No one can see us here." She stripped and stood naked before him, and he saw every detail. He was thrilled, not so much by her body, which he had seen so many times before, but by the fact that he saw it here in the storm shelter. No one else had ever been here before. "I do feel like a virgin, here."

He kissed her, and she kissed him, and they sank down on the stone floor and made love. It was glorious.

Then he guided her so that she was able to make her own storm shelter that no one else needed to see or even know about. She had been sexually molested as a small child, in the woodshed, and not even understood the nature of it until years later; then she had buried it, embarrassed. Now that memory served to hide whatever other secrets she might have. But, to erase the ugly smell of it, she took Wetzel into that woodshed and made love to him there. Now it was a place with a pleasant memory that she would not mind visiting again.

"Thank you, Wetzel, for this marvelous gift," she said. "This is my place of restored virginity. I will always be a virgin here. Only you know better."

"I know no such thing. I love you, my virgin." He kissed her again, loving her, and she melted in his embrace. In her mind she had indeed become virginal here, and that was what truly counted.

Then they emerged and found themselves in her bed in her house, pleasantly embraced. That closeness, physically and emotionally, had enabled them to achieve the visit and construction. To make her a secret virgin.

"You know, I think now I could stay with you, because—"

"No," she said gently. "Let the fond illusion be our secret." And of course she was right.

In the morning the trail remained. He transformed, touched her fondly with his horn, and marched onto the trail. He did not look back, knowing he would see her tears.

CHAPTER 3: TRAIL MATES

The trail soon left the village behind. It wound through a forest that was at first similar to the one he knew, but gradually became dissimilar. Still distracted by the memory of Weava, so deserving a woman yet ultimately not for him, he paid scant attention. He hadn't even thought to bring any clothing or pack any supplies. He could go back for them, but did not want to disrupt the parting they had already managed. He would make do.

Where did the trail lead? Weava had spoken of the Amoeba, a creature that spanned the whole of existence. It seemed it offered the trail only to individuals needed for a mission. He had no idea what such a mission could be, and less idea what beetle juice meant. Some sort of beverage? A sexual reference? Or was it a code for something completely alien? Or a gross cosmic joke?

Then he became aware of human minds. There was a village ahead. That was a relief; someone there might have a notion what he was here for.

He trotted up to the village, but the villagers ignored him, continuing about their assorted businesses. He could tell from their minds that they were aware of him, but determined not to interact with him unless he initiated it. It seemed that was Amoeba policy. He could also tell that they had been through a significant experience recently, some kind of threat they had had to fight off, and they were still making repairs. He could not learn more without prying unduly.

Then he spied a group of four people camped at the far edge of the village, somewhat apart from it. An old man, a young man, and two young women. One of them was ordinary, the other a striking beauty; neither was a virgin. They saw him coming, and were eager to interact with him. These were people he needed to converse with; they evidently knew why he was here. They were members of an experienced team, and they had been waiting for another member. That would be him. It was clarifying as their assorted thoughts radiated.

He walked on through the village, approaching the foursome. The two women gazed at his form and loved it. That was normal for non-virgins. But it reminded him that he was in equine form. If we wanted to talk with these people he had to revert to human form. He did so, coming to a halt before them. "I see that you are the members of the team I am supposed to join," he said, evincing more dramatic confidence than he felt. If they were not such a team, he would be at a loss.

They were silent, still assessing him. "I am sure we will get along capitally," he continued, again hoping it was true. "I am Wetzel." He glanced at the women, who did not know he could read their thoughts, and were thinking rather nakedly, especially the pretty one. "Thank you for your honest appreciation of my physical equine and manly qualities, ladies."

Now the pretty one spoke, and he picked up her name. She was a vampire! A were-bat with a taste for blood and sex. That was a surprise. "We didn't speak."

"Ah, but you did, Vanja." Then he had to explain. "You see, I am telepathic. More precisely, I am a telepathic were-unicorn." He smiled. "We are a rare breed. I presume it was for my ability to read minds that I was summoned here, though I did have other qualities." He looked again at the women, who both blushed. It seemed that in their cultures women were not supposed to have raw sexual desire, and seldom voiced it. Their unprotected minds were thus an embarrassment.

Meanwhile the young man was dismayed. It seemed that he had had access to both women, and now feared competition. He wondered what they had gotten into. He needed reassurance, as Wetzel did not want to have to deal with a jealous husband or equivalent. "Perhaps I can answer that too, Tod," he said, naming the man. "There is a concept in my mind that I presume stems from the Amoeba and relates to our mission." Again, this was partly guesswork that he hoped to have confirmed.

"A concept?" the man asked. He was evidently the leader of this group. "What is it?"

"Beetle Juice. I am as perplexed by it as you are, but there it is."

"We will surely be finding out soon," the older man said. His name turned out to be Wizard, and it seemed that was literal. He could actually perform magic.

"Bug juice," Vanja the Vampire said. "That could be considered a form of blood."

"Or simply a squished insect," the young man, Tod, said.

"First things first," the luscious vampire said. She had voluminous black hair that flounced about her shoulders and breasts, contrasting red pupils, and of course visible fangs. "You must be worn from your journey here, and there is much we will need to tell you. Why don't I just get you alone for a while and bring you up to date, Wetzel?"

Both men smiled, agreeing, knowing her nature, and the other woman, after a pause, agreed too. It seemed that Vanja would be the one to initiate him into their group. He was amenable.

"Your other form is a unicorn," Vanja said. "I'm a girl, and girls love horses. Similar species. Would you let me ride you?"

Such a thing had not occurred to him. Be ridden like an animal? Yet he wanted to get along with these people, and if this was the price of her favor, he could do it.

And that will alleviate your nakedness, which is embarrassing Veee, she thought.

Oh. He transformed.

She stood beside him, then jumped, sprawling onto his back. She swung a leg over, grabbed his mane, and sat up, steadying herself. "I'm not an experienced rider. You can readily dump me off if you have a mind to. I won't be hurt; I'll simply go to my bat form and hover."

Now he realized something else. She wore no clothing. What had looked like clothing was pigmented skin. He felt her bare thighs against his skin, all the way up to her crotch. That was a sexual turn-on. She was no virgin, but she was certainly interesting, and would do for a sexual partner. He stepped forward carefully so that she would not be dislodged.

I assume you are reading my mind, she thought without speaking. *You know I want to have sex with you. That's why I'm touching you in a way I know you are noticing. There's a private glade up this path where we can stop and do it. Then we'll talk.*

He could not speak in this form, but he could respond. He

walked along the path her mind indicated. She was correct about his noticing her warm thighs and crotch. He was eager to have sex with her, more so than with any non-virginal stranger he could remember.

We're two of a kind, transformers, just different types. We should get along. But tell me by nodding your head: is it true about unicorns and virgins?

He nodded his head.

But you can enjoy regular women too?

He nodded again. He was already enjoying their physical contact.

"Then we'll get along," she said, reverting to audible speech now that she had confirmed the telepathic mode. "Now I have some points to make while I have you muzzled. I'm no virgin, but I can seduce any man in short order when I try. I will be happy to demonstrate with you. Meanwhile I'll answer your most likely question: yes, it's true about vampires and blood. But as a general rule I don't take the blood of friends, and I do have an alternate way to get the equivalent: a man's semen bolsters me similarly. So when you have sex with me, you are actually feeding me. I don't need a lot, a few drops will do, it's a hormonal thing, but I do need it regularly. So I will be after you for sex every night, and not just because you are one magnetically virile stud. If you don't like that, simply tell me; I do have other sources." She squeezed her thighs against his hide suggestively.

Wetzel walked on, not demurring. It was interesting how she was managing him, effectively silencing him while she made her presentation. He liked her, and she was indeed sexually interesting, especially for a vampire. His fantasy research had indicated that vampires could take sex or leave it; her ability to use it in lieu of blood was not in the literature he had seen.

"Another thing," she continued. "We are a team, and we stand by each other, to the death if need be. You join us, we'll stand by you, and expect you to support us similarly. We'll be your friends. It is no casual commitment; the Amoeba brought us together for a purpose, and we need to know we can depend on each other. But apart from that, the other woman, Veee, is my friend. I don't want her hurt. Anyone who hurts her will be my enemy." Her mood darkened, and it was clear that she was neither joking nor bluffing. "I'm not suggesting that you would do so deliberately, but you could do so unintentionally, simply because you don't yet know her well enough. Reading her immediate mind won't necessarily suffice. She has had wide involuntary sexual experience, but now is in a voluntary relationship with Tod, and is becoming her own woman. They love each other and will marry in due course. You could surely seduce her, because of your magical appeal to women, but she would thereafter feel guilty and be hurt. She wants to be true to Tod. It's a cultural thing. So I ask you, I beg you, do not have sex with her. You can be her friend—she makes the best possible friend—but leave her alone sexually. I am not trying to reserve you for myself; you can have sex with anyone else, and I suspect you will, just as I do with any man who takes my fancy, including especially Tod. Veee and I share him, for now; that's complicated to explain briefly. She's not the jealous type. But Veee alone you should spare."

Wetzel walked on. Vanja's mind buttressed her words; she was making sense in this context. He would try to honor that request.

They came to the glade. He transformed back to human form, and sure enough, Vanja transformed simultaneously to her bat form, hovered momentarily, then landed on his shoulder.

"I have heard you, vocally and mentally," he said. "I will treat your friend carefully. Because she is not a virgin, I should be able to hold off."

She jumped off his shoulder, transformed, and landed neatly on her feet before him, now completely nude in appearance. She put her arms about him, drawing close so that her belly and breasts pressed against him. She had the most provocative figure he had ever seen. "One other thing," she murmured, smiling to flash her fangs. "I don't bite when making love, unless requested." Then she kissed him and drew him down on the grass, wrapping her legs about his hips. He was in her and climaxing immediately; she was indeed good at seduction and at sex.

"Now more detail," she said briskly as they lay still clasped. "Exactly what is it with unicorns and virgins? Are you really helpless before a virgin?"

"It's a liability of the form. My passion is for a virgin, but the moment I have sex with her I lose further romantic interest. I can enjoy sex with any woman, but I can love only a virgin. I want to love and marry and have a family, but my wife must be a continuing virgin. It's not just her body; she must be virginal in her mind too. I know that's impossible. I took the trail in the hope that somewhere, somehow, there is an answer for me."

"So if you find the right virgin, your life is complete?"

"Hardly. I am completely smitten by any virgin I meet; she can make me do almost anything. Until she stops being virginal."

"So, if we encounter an enemy virgin, one who wishes us ill, we will need to protect you from her, odd as that sounds?"

"Yes. I cannot say no to a virgin. So I am not looking for a virgin as such, so much as THE virgin who will fulfill my life, imaginary as she may be."

"I don't know enough about the Amoeba to say, but it is my impression that it does try to satisfy the ones it summons. So maybe there is an answer for you, though I can't imagine what."

"I hope so," he said fervently.

"Okay, I believe I have introduced myself. Next you should get to know Tod. He's the leader of our team. He'll need to know your capabilities so he can organize the mission."

"What *is* the mission?"

"We don't know. Just that it relates to beetle juice, thanks to your information. That's typical of the Amoeba; it doesn't tell you, but in due course does show the way. We can be sure it will be a challenge that utilizes all of us, though maybe not in exactly the ways we expect."

They got up and walked back toward the village. Wetzel noticed that her painted clothing had reappeared. Too bad he could not do the same. "Thank you for the information," he said.

"Thank you for the ride."

He smiled. "Who thanks whom for the sex?"

She returned the smile. "It's a draw. We both desperately wanted it. We're a close match both in being half-humans and in our keen sexuality. There will be many other times."

"There will be," he agreed.

They rejoined the other three. "I am turning Wetzel over to you, Tod, for background on the Amoeba and our organization as a team." She flashed a smile. "And yes, he *is* a stud."

"Let's take a walk," Tod said. He was a fit brown-haired man of pleasant disposition.

"First get him some trunks," Veee said. She was embarrassed by his nakedness, though also admiring it.

Tod rummaged in his things and came up with a pair of undershorts. Wetzel put them on. "I did not think to bring clothing of my own," he said. "When I transform suddenly, it is hard on clothing."

"Veee will surely design you something feasible."

"I will," Veee said.

They walked along the same path as before. "The Amoeba is a remarkable entity," Tod said. His mind was well informed and surprisingly powerful; he was much more of a person than his appearance or attitude suggested. "The trails are actually its pseudopods, extending beyond our imagination. We are in the Amoeba, and it facilitates our association."

"*In* it?" Wetzel asked, surprised. "I assumed it was controlling the trail from some other vantage."

"Not so. Everything you see here is part of the Amoeba. It provides a mutually compatible environment so that all of us are physically comfortable, when we might not be in each other's frames. It also enables us to converse with each other, though our individual languages may be quite different. Your telepathy may enable you to relate to foreign cultures on your own, however."

"I am not sure of that," Wetzel said. "I have no prior experience with foreign cultures. But it may be so. That might be why I was offered the trail."

"We may find out, in due course. We each have special abilities and traits. It seems the Amoeba is essentially mindless, but senses what it needs and goes after it. That may not be what we think. Our prior fifth member was Bem, an alien blob. But there's a more immediate aspect. You have not eaten anything here?"

"I have not," Wetzel agreed.

"There is a sickness that comes the first time a person eats on the trail. We have all suffered it. It occurs once, then not again. First you vomit, then you get the implacable chills that it seems only close personal contact can ward off. Your best bet is to eat very little, wait for the siege, then let the girls bundle with you under a blanket."

"Both women?"

"Two are warmer than one. It seems to be not merely physical."

This could be awkward. "Vanja told me to leave Veee alone, sexually. I intend to do that. I should not be put artificially close to her. It is difficult for me to resist sexual temptation."

"I appreciate your caution. But when you are sick, you will not be sexually inclined."

"She said that you and Veee may marry."

"Yes, we hope to. But here on the trail it is open territory, sexually. We are not possessive of each other. If you and Veee wish to indulge you can, as long as the desire is mutual. I do so with both women, sometimes simultaneously." He smiled. "That can be quite an experience."

"Vanja said Veee would feel guilty, and thus be hurt. I do not wish to do that."

"That is purely up to the two of you. Vanja is very much her own woman, and Veee is getting there."

"I have normally had sex with any woman who wanted it, and in my proximity all do, except for virgins. I fear Veee would also. It is better simply to keep us apart. I do not want to be a divisive influence in this group."

"This is an understanding you must come to with Veee. It is not my prerogative to tell either of you what to do in this respect. If there is an emergency we need to handle, such as a charging monster, then I will expect all of you to heed what I say. But that is the extent of it."

The man was unusually tolerant, and his mind echoed his words. Still, Wetzel intended to stay clear. "Maybe it is time for me to eat something local, and handle my ensuing illness. Then we can consider what other limits exist."

"Good idea," Tod agreed.

Wetzel paused to pick a single blue berry. "Will this do?"

"Yes. But don't eat it yet. Wait until the girls can help you."

Wetzel was bemused, but decided to play it through. These were nice people, open and honest, and he liked them already. He might have been selected to fill a specific role the Amoeba required, friendship no object, but the prospect of associating with them appealed.

"One other thing," Tod said. "The words you picked up, beetle juice. Were they capitalized?"

"I believe they were," Wetzel said, surprised.

"That suggests that my conjecture about a squished bug was wrong. There is another interpretation. Betelgeuse."

"A giant red star?" Wetzel asked, picking it up from the man's mind.

"Beetle Juice capitalized is a nickname in my culture for the star. In my language, which may not be what we are using here, the two phrasings sound similar."

"But that is far away from here."

"The Amoeba extends everywhere, and neither time nor distance is any barrier to it. The next village down the trail could be in the vicinity of Betelgeuse."

"That being the case, why wasn't Betelgeuse put into my mind, instead of Beetle Juice?"

"I don't know. There must be a reason. It can be complicated to figure out the simple mind of the Amoeba."

"So it seems," Wetzel agreed, smiling. He was gaining respect for Tod; the man had a competent way of thinking.

They returned to the group. "Wetzel will eat a berry," Tod said.

"We'll get the wash basin," Vanja said.

"And the blanket," Veee added.

"I'm not cold," Wetzel protested.

They merely smiled. "Eat your berry," Tod said.

Wetzel ate it. It was delicious.

"Meanwhile, you can get to know Veee," Tod said. He and Wizard departed.

Veee stepped close. "There is something about you."

"It is my sexual appeal," Wetzel said. "It is my nature to be attracted to virgins, while experienced women are attracted to me. While I am unable to truly love any non-virgins, I can enjoy sex with them. However, I think it best if you and I do not indulge in that manner."

"Why not?" Her interest was intensifying.

Wetzel glanced at Vanja, but she was silent. Even her mind was guarded. She had said her say and was leaving it to him.

"It is my understanding that you prefer to be true to Tod, whom you will marry. In my culture, married women are not normally encouraged to indulge sexually elsewhere. It happens, but is frowned on."

"This is true for me too," Veee said. "Yet I am tempted." Indeed she was; her mind was churning.

"You might be tempted to eat a tasty berry, too," he said. "But would not if you knew it was poisonous."

"You are poisonous?"

"A sexual relationship with me could poison your association with Tod."

"I do not blame him for having sex with Vanja. He would not blame me for having it with you." This was true, but her feelings were seriously mixed.

"Not because of him," Wetzel said carefully. "Because of you. You would hate to yield to the illicit temptation of the moment."

"You're reading my mind!"

"I am," he agreed.

"You know you could take me this instant."

"Please, your burgeoning passion incites my own. It is like a fire spreading. Get away from me." His erection was showing within the shorts.

She did not move. "I know I should. I know I'll condemn myself tomorrow. But right now I can't help myself. I want you."

"And I want you. But we must not. I would feel as guilty as you."

She reached for him. "Then stop me, because I can't stop myself."

Vanja remained impassive. She would not intervene.

That gave him an inspiration. "There is a turn-off my people use to prevent rape. I will teach it to you."

"This isn't rape."

"Yes it is. Of both of us. We don't want to have sex, but are being overwhelmed by the immediate passion."

Veee nodded, seeing it. "Hurry."

"It is a thought, a mind set. It is like a—a very bad smell. You must think of sex as utterly disgusting, abhorrent, repulsive."

"But it's not." But there was a hint of something in her memory. Before she had taken the trail.

He pounced on it. "Think of a man you don't like forcing sex on you. Of rape. You hate the notion, but he doesn't care about that. He means to have it despite your aversion."

Her memory expanded. She had had sex like that. "Ugh."

"That's it. Magnify that feeling."

She did. She was fighting the man mentally, not physically, because she didn't dare. That made it worse. The thought of his hard member penetrating her made her sick.

"Yes," Wetzel said. "With my telepathy I pick up that thought, and it turns me off." He pulled down the shorts to reveal his member gone limp.

"I'll be damned," Vanja murmured appreciatively.

Then Wetzel suddenly vomited. It was messy, splattering himself and the ground before him.

"The sickness!" Veee said. "Drink water, wash it out." She held up a jug.

Wetzel gulped water, then immediately puked it out again. He heaved until he was dry. He was glad he had eaten only one berry!

Vanja brought a damp cloth and wiped him off. "Take off your shorts," she said.

The women helped him get out of the shorts, and completed his cleanup. Then they took him to a small tent they had and made him lie down on a blanket. "But I'm not cold," he protested.

Then he shivered. It was as though a chill winter wind had caught him naked, only the wind was from inside him.

The women stripped and joined him on the blanket, pressing tightly against him from either side. They drew the blanket over them all. Their bodies were warm, and that was an immense comfort. Tod was right: he felt no sexual inclination. All he wanted was to somehow escape the coldness. He realized that it wasn't actually physical; it was psychic, and it could be abated only by living energy transfused from other bodies. They were providing that, and he was grateful. It came from their minds as much as from their bodies, buoying him immeasurably.

He wasn't sure how much time had passed, but knew he was recovering. The women remained bound to him, sharing their heat. "I think I am better now," he said.

"We'll know when you're better," Vanja said.

He was curious. "How?"

She reached down to tweak his limp penis. "When this signals us."

He had to laugh. They were both nude and pressing everything against him, and he felt all of it, yet he had no ambition for sex. It was a novel experience.

Before long, however, his member did stir. Then they let go of him. Veee brought another pair of shorts and he put them on. He remained physically weak. "Thank you for warning me, so that I ate only a token amount. Thank you for taking care of me. I don't know how I would have handled it alone."

"We understand," Vanja said. "We have been there."

"I was sick for what seemed like hours," Veee said. "Tod saved me."

"That was when the two of you bonded," Wetzel said.

"I suppose it was. I liked him from then on."

Vanja put away the blanket. "I will leave the two of you to it." She walked away, her clothing forming around her.

"The way you showed me to turn off sex," Veee said. "I wish I had known it earlier in life."

"It works only with telepaths. They have to read your mind. But keep it handy."

"The only one I can use it against is you."

"And you should. That way we won't do anything we will regret." He glanced at her, realizing that she remained nude. "Use it now. And put on your clothing."

"Oh." She summoned the turn-off mood, and dressed. "I suppose if I ever do encounter another telepathic male, it could be useful. But how will I know he's reading my mind?"

Wetzel explained how to pick up on the feather touch, and drilled her on it, until she could tell the moment he snooped. She was an apt learner, quite intelligent.

"But I can't actually stop him from reading my mind," she said. "So if he wanted to know something I wanted to keep secret, I would be helpless."

And Wetzel knew he would have to share the secret of his storm cellar with her and the others. Because they might indeed encounter telepathy, and have to preserve private information. That might even be the reason he had been summoned. "There is a way. But it may be awkward to set up."

She was interested. But there was a problem, as he had feared. The storm shelter had to be tied to something she wanted no one else to know, and she would have to let *him* know. "I think I'd rather have the rape," she said candidly.

"Then you don't have to make the shelter," he said. "It's just our guess that there will be other telepaths."

"I think I do have to make it. But let me mull it a while. There's something I would like to know about you, if you are willing to tell me."

"Virgins," he said.

She shook her head. "I keep forgetting that you can read my mind! Yes. I think you said you are attracted to them. Are they similarly attracted to you?"

"No. They know I will destroy their virginity, changing them forever, and are wary. Whereas experienced women have less sexual reticence and are attracted to my animal magnetism. So I am forever pursuing the only women who don't want me, while being pursued by the ones I can't love. This is quite apart from merit; I know there are many worthy women who could make me happy, if only I didn't have this thing about virginity. It's not logical, it's magical, a geis, a foolish obligation of honor without much honor in it."

"That is your tragedy."

"It is what really motivated me to take the trail. The hope that somewhere I can find that oxymoron, a perpetually virginal sexual partner. A woman I can love, marry, and make a family with. I fear it's impossible, but that's my dream."

"We will help you find her."

"A pregnant virgin is a contradiction in terms. Her body has to know she has had sexual experience, and her mind and emotion will know it too."

"Are there levels of virginity? I mean, you have not had sex with me, so aren't I a virgin to you in that respect?"

Wetzel hadn't considered that before. "I suppose there are. My first experience with a woman is more interesting than my second, so there may be some magic there, as it were. You are indeed more appealing to me than you would be after sex." He thought of Weava, a significant exception, but preferred not to go into that.

"Is it your mind or hers that counts most?"

"Hers. I read the virginity in her mind, or the relative novelty if she is not a virgin, and react to that."

"So we can be better friends if we do not have sex."

"Yes, actually." Then he found himself telling her about Weava after all, because he knew from her mind that she would understand and sympathize, and he needed that.

She did. "I like that woman," Veee said. "You should have married her."

"She wouldn't let me. She wanted what was best for me, and felt unworthy."

"Unworthy! She is the most worthy person I have heard about."

"Oh, yes," he said, and the emotion welled up and overcame him. He found himself in Veee's embrace, being comforted. And realized that if Weava was the most worthy person, Veee might be the next most worthy. Vanja had recognized her as the best possible friend. Vanja was right.

"Weava made her storm shelter," Veee said. "I must be guided by her."

Wetzel was surprised; he had not seen that coming in her

thoughts. She had evidently made a sudden decision. "As you wish. I will have to see your secret, but I promise not to reveal it elsewhere. You will have to trust me on this."

"I do," she said. That was another thing he liked about her she trusted others because she was trustworthy herself. "I will show you my secret. Read my mind."

Her mind flashed back to her early life. He became an invisible observer.

There was a group of children on the playground. Seeing no boys, Veee took the initiative. "Let's play hide and guess," she said.

The other girls merely looked at her, or beyond her. Realizing that something was amiss, she turned.

There was a boy standing behind her. She had not seen him approach. She had just committed a serious social blunder, taking the initiative when a boy was present. It was accidental, but appalling. "Oh!" she cried, and ran away in shame.

As it happened, the boy did not tell on her, and neither did the other girls. But they all knew. She became a de facto pariah, no one's friend. She could not bear to be with them any more, and busied herself doing other things.

Not long thereafter her family moved to another village. This put her into a new group that did not know her history. She was able to relate to the children and bury the memory. She was careful never to commit such a blunder again. The episode was lost in the welter of other childish experiences. But it remained her deepest private shame.

Wetzel did not comment in the merit of her case, though it would not have been anything shameful or even remarkable in his own culture where girls and boys had other concerns. The shame was real to her, and that was what counted. He showed her how to frame the guilty memory, encapsulating it, so that it was no longer part of her conscious thoughts. He showed her how she could mentally latch on to other memories, haul them into that capsule, and thus bury them too. A passing telepath might freely read her mind, but would not be aware of the storm shelter. It was so secret that even its existence was secret. That made it truly effective.

"Thank you," Veee said. "You have given me three gifts: detection of the feather touch, repulsion of sex by a telepathic male, and the storm shelter. I can offer you nothing in return, unless—"

"No!" he said. "No sex. You are giving me something invaluable in return: your friendship and understanding."

"I will try to find your permanent virgin," she said. "That will be a better return gift."

He let it go. Veee did not realize how much he already valued her support. Perhaps in time she would.

She passed him along to the last member of their team, Wizard. He was an old man, white bearded, with a conical cap, slight of stature but phenomenal of magic ability. Wetzel had not actually seen it in action, but the others had. Wizard's thoughts were too complicated to read readily. "Yes, I really do do magic," he said. "Here is a sample of the least energy-consuming variety, illusion."

A giant two-footed creature appeared, stomping toward them with a baleful glare. Wetzel was alarmed; it looked as if the thing could bash them both into oblivion with one swoop of its hairy muscular arm. Then it dissolved into the shape of a small bird, which flew away.

"Completely unreal," Wizard said. "But useful in the event of an attack by an ignorant warrior. Such a bluff might abate the threat right there."

"Bluff? Suppose the soldier catches on, and ignores it?"

Wizard smiled. "Illusion can be deadly. Do you see that tree?"

"A solid one," Wetzel agreed. "But a tree is readily avoided."

"Observe." The tree vanished. In its place was a pleasantly winding forest path.

Wetzel appreciated the trap. "The soldier could walk right into that tree, not seeing it. But still, that might not hurt him. It might just make him mad."

"Observe." Now a maiden appeared with a shape much like Vanja's. She looked toward them and her mouth opened in a silent scream. She ran, her dress catching on a snag and tearing off to reveal her flashing buttocks.

"He would charge after her, lest she escape," Wetzel said. "And run into the tree at full speed. He could knock himself out."

"Illusion can as readily mask a pit. Even after people catch on, they dare not proceed rapidly, lest they run afoul of concealed natural barriers."

"I agree. This is impressive magic."

"I can also do telekinesis, that is, move things without touching them physically, by magic. And fire bombing. But these require much personal energy and quickly exhaust me. Perhaps my most useful incidental talent is scrying. That is, fathoming the nature of a person or situation so that we do not approach either entirely blindly."

"Did you see me coming, before I first joined your party?"

"No, I need to be close to the subject to scry it. But I can scry you now, if you are amenable."

"Go ahead. It will better acquaint you with me."

Wizard touched Wetzel's hand. "Ah yes, the virginity issue." He paused. "Now that's a surprise."

"Something in my background?"

"Something in your foreground. Normally my scrying reveals the salient qualities of a person's past, but in your case it seems to be the future." He paused again, concentrating. "No, merely your present, but it points the way to your future. There is a virgin."

"There are many virgins," Wetzel said. "That's not my problem."

"*Your* virgin. The one you can love, marry, and beget a family with."

"She exists?" Wetzel asked, wary of some cruel misunderstanding.

"She exists in the Betelgeuse region. She is young, pretty, and nice, but may be unrecognizable. You may encounter her and not know her for what she is. You must be alert to fathom her nature and make her your own."

"I should be able to identify her by reading her mind."

"Not so. My scry indicates that you will not find her that way."

"She's immune to telepathy?"

"No. Merely not identifiable thereby."

"I don't understand."

"Neither do I. There's always the chance that the scry is false."

"In which case there's no virgin."

Wizard nodded. "It happens, but seldom. It seems more likely that we merely do not properly understand the scry."

"How do we properly understand seeming nonsense?"

"I am minded of Tod's described computer-assisted game of cards. That seems like nonsense to me. Read my mind."

Wetzel tried. The concept was of some kind of sophisticated machine that enabled a person to play cards and warned him when he made a bad move. Wetzel could not comprehend the machine or the game, but did get the message: the warning could prevent a person from making a bad move, without informing him of the correct move. Sometimes it seemed as if there were no good moves, yet somehow they existed and could be found with appropriate diligence.

"So there may be an unrecognizable virgin I can marry and have children with," Wetzel said. "Without suffering loss of love in the process."

"That is the indication."

"So it would be a bad move to give up my quest for her. She may seem like a contradiction in terms, a virgin birthing babies, but I can find her and win her if I truly believe in her."

"So it seems."

"It sounds like self delusion. An ordinary woman that I choose to believe is virginal even after I impregnate her. I am not into delusion."

Wizard smiled. "You were not into illusion, either, before I demonstrated it. It may be that your framework of beliefs constitutes a kind of illusion, so that you are unable to see the reality beyond them."

"I have not walked into any invisible trees lately."

"Illusions don't have to be apparent to have force. Have you considered that your quest for a virgin may be a wrong direction?"

"I left the most worthy of women behind, in my quest for a fantasy woman. That seems likely to be a wrong direction. Yet it was a course she urged on me."

Wizard nodded. "Therefore, rightly or wrongly, you must follow this course until it is resolved. My experience with the Amoeba suggests that it does not make empty promises. There may be a virgin, if we have the wit to find her."

"We?"

"You have joined our team. You will assist us to the best of your ability. We will assist you to the best of ours. Maybe you can't locate your virgin alone, but we can. We will try."

"Even if you don't believe she exists?"

"I believe she exists, perhaps in some alternate universe. The Amoeba reaches into alternate universes." Wizard paused again, thinking. "Our prior member, Bem, had a problem when its society was threatened. It turned out that what it learned here on the trail enabled it to reform its thinking and navigate the crisis. It may be that you need similarly to modify your thinking, in order to be able to appreciate your virgin."

Wetzel knew that Wizard was not trying to deceive him or cause him to believe in nonsense. There had to be something. "I will try," he agreed.

CHAPTER 4: DEFENSE

—∼—

"It is time to get moving," Tod declared.

Nobody argued, though Wetzel realized that Tod did not know where to go. He simply had confidence that the Amoeba would guide them to their destination. It seemed it had before. They packed their meager belongings.

"I can carry them, in my unicorn form," Wetzel said. "Or a person." He had come to terms with the idea of being a beast of burden. If that was the true reason the team needed him, it was worth it.

"Wizard," Tod said.

"I don't know how to ride a steed," Wizard protested.

"Chances are we'll make better time if you are not afoot," Tod told him. "You also need to save your energy in case we walk into trouble on the trail."

"Point taken," Wizard said. "But the day is late, and we have information about each other to assimilate. We should start in the morning."

"Yes."

They had a meal of local fruits and some kind of orange meat that Wetzel did not inquire about. In his human form he could eat things he could not as a unicorn. Then Vanja unpacked a blanket and brought it to Wetzel. "You know the drill, lover."

They lay in a glade and she had at him three times before concluding that enough was enough and dropping off to sleep. Then he slept also. But in his mind the woman he embraced was Weava. How could he have left her? Yet if there really was a special virgin . . .

In the morning they ate, repacked, and set off. Wetzel assumed unicorn form and carried Wizard on a makeshift straw saddle. Tod led the way, followed by Veee, and then Wetzel and Wizard, with Vanja in bat form perched on Wetzel's head. That was all right as long as she didn't poop on his mane. They moved briskly along a trail leading from the village. Tod was right: the frail old man would not have kept the pace.

"Here is the thing," Wizard said. "I do not like seeming like an invalid, and could walk at this rate assisted by magic. But it is best that I save my energy for some possible emergency. We are going to a new region and there may be dangers along the way. The Amoeba does not ensure our safety, merely that we are competent to accomplish the mission; we have to see to our own survival."

The bat abruptly took off, flew into the brush, and landed on a creature Wetzel hadn't seen. It was a rabbit. It jumped, alarmed, but the bat's eyeteeth were already puncturing its neck. The vampire was feeding.

In a moment she let go and flew up. The rabbit bounded away, not visibly hurt. There had been time for only a sip of its blood. As Vanja had said, she did not need much, but did need it or the equivalent regularly.

The bat circled, evidently checking the local scene, then returned to perch again on Wetzel's head. *I need even less in bat form*, she thought. *If I wanted to hurt someone, I'd do it in human form and take more than a token.*

He was glad to have seen it. It filled out his awareness of her as a vampire.

Veee sniffed. "Wolfkey," she said.

The bat immediately took off and circled, exploring the vicinity. Wetzel read the concept in Veee's mind, which she organized for his information. A wolfkey was what seemed to be a crossbreed creature, part wolf, part monkey, all predator. They liked to go after travelers on the trails, as travelers tended to be more isolated and have fewer defensive resources, thus being easier prey. The wolfkeys had been largely cleaned out of the area where Wetzel had joined the team, but now they were beyond that region. This was bad news.

The bat returned, transforming to human. "A pack of six or eight of them," she reported. "They have winded us and are coming up from behind. They'll be here in fifteen minutes."

Tod halted and turned to face them. "Any convenient place for defense?"

"I saw none close enough."

"Then I'll have to use my gun." Tod formed a picture in his mind for Wetzel to read, showing a small object he could hold in his hand that propelled bits of metal rapidly forward with lethal effect.

Veee came to help Wizard dismount. "What's your take on this, Wetzel?" she asked.

Wetzel changed to manform. "You do not need the gun weapon. I can deal with the type of creature your minds describe."

"Your horn?" She was averting her gaze, not comfortable with his nakedness. It gave her ideas she preferred to avoid.

"It is a weapon. I have dealt with rogue dogs in the past. The action is not pretty, but I can handle several."

"Six or eight?"

"Two at a time. If more attack me simultaneously it would get ugly, but with my larger mass I could take out enough so that the rest of you could handle what is left."

Veee drew her knife. "We will do that."

"I can help," Wizard said. "I will watch from a safe distance, spotting all the wolfkeys in my mind. Read my mind and you will see a map, so that you know exactly where each is without looking directly. None will surprise you."

"That will do," Wetzel agreed. He transformed back to unicorn form.

Vanja became the bat and flew up. *They are coming*.

Wetzel braced himself for a fast charge, and waited.

Now. And the animals appeared, running swiftly along the trail. *They are grouped two by two, seven in all*, Wizard thought, showing the formation in his mind.

Wetzel charged, horn lowered. He speared the left creature, whipped up his head, and flung its carcass over his back. Even as he did that, he raised his right hoof and clubbed the other on the shoulder. It dropped to the ground, seriously injured.

The next two wolfkeys hurriedly braked. Then they backed off. They were not afraid — Wetzel read that in their limited minds — but neither were they foolhardy. They were up against more than they had anticipated.

Wetzel lowered his blood-soaked horn and strode toward them. They quickly turned tail and ran, followed by the others.

Vanja landed and transformed. "Now that's what I call a good show," she said approvingly. "I'll put this one out of its misery." She dropped down beside the injured one and put her face to its neck. In a moment it expired; Wetzel felt the release as her toxin stopped its heart. That was one vampire he did not want as an enemy!

Veee produced a towel and wiped off Wetzel's horn. "You can rinse it when we next find water," she said.

But there was no need. Wetzel simply plunged his horn into the sand, and it emerged reasonably clean.

Tod and Veee butchered the two bodies and packed away the meat for future use. Then Wizard mounted the unicorn again and they resumed travel.

"I could have levitated the wolfkeys so that they floated and had no traction, becoming easy targets," Wizard said. "But I would have had to be dangerously close to them to do it, and it would have seriously depleted my personal energy. Your way was better, and more impressive."

Wetzel was glad he didn't need to answer. He was satisfied to have proven himself in this manner.

The trail ascended a steepening slope. Tod hardly slowed, and Veee kept the pace. "Veee is a sturdy woman," Wizard said. "She carried me cross-country during our prior mission."

At the crest of the hill there was a fork. Tod hesitated, then bore to the right. This was a lesser trail heading down into a jungle.

Wetzel, wondering why Tod had not taken the main trail, extended his telepathic awareness. And caught something. DANGER. He halted.

"Something you sense?" Wizard asked, sliding off to land on the ground. Vanja dropped similarly, transforming to her woman form.

Now Wetzel transformed. "I can't read minds at a distance, but I can get a hint," he said. "There is something dangerous down that side trail. We should not go there."

"I'll tell Tod," Vanja said. She became the bat and flew off after Tod and Veee, who were already out of sight.

"Too far for me to scry," Wizard said. "But your alarm is surely well taken."

The bat returned, becoming Vanja. "I intercepted them, told them to stop, but they ignored me," she said. "Something has hold of them."

"A mind predator," Wetzel said. "Broadcasting a summoning signal. I'll stop them."

"But it didn't affect me," Vanja said.

"It is affecting me," Wizard said. "Now that I'm standing alone. Maybe it orients on full humans, so you and Wetzel are immune. Go and stop them. Block them physically if you have to. Carry them back here where the signal is weaker. Then we can retreat the way we came, getting out of range. I dare not go with you. It is all I can do to stand still instead of yielding to the urge. But I will try to devise a defense we can use to abate this menace."

"This way, lover," Vanja said, returning to bat form and flying away. Wetzel transformed to unicorn form and galloped after her.

The distance was not far. In moments they overhauled the man and woman who were still marching down the hill. Wetzel circled around them, then blocked the path ahead of them with his mass.

Vanja became human. "Go back, you fools!" she cried. "You're not going where you want to go!"

The two did not heed her. They pushed almost blindly against Wetzel as if not seeing him.

"Haul them out of here," Vanja said. She bent to grasp Veee around the middle and heave her up onto Wetzel's rump. Then she wrestled Tod around similarly. Neither person resisted her, but neither cooperated; they seemed to be unaware of her. Whatever had hold on their minds took their whole attention.

"Move!" she said to Wetzel. "I'll try to keep them on you."

He stepped carefully forward, carrying the two bodies sprawled on his back. They started to slide off, but Vanja shoved them back on. He took another step, and a third.

It was slow and clumsy, but they made progress up the hill. They came into sight of Wizard, who was locked in place, not going forward but also not able to retreat. "Keep moving!" Wizard called. "The hold will weaken with distance."

Then something changed. Wetzel felt it in his mind. The unseen monster had become aware that it was being balked, and was reassessing its tactics. Wetzel wanted to warn Vanja and Wizard, but would have had to change forms, and that would stop moving the others.

The monster reoriented. Now Wetzel felt the compulsion. He tried to resist it, but it overpowered him. He turned slowly around and started back down the hill, toward the monster.

"Oh no!" Vanja exclaimed. Then she too reoriented.

The half-humans were not immune, merely different. Now the monster had found their range and captured their minds.

Tod and Veee slid off Wetzel's back. They found their footing and resumed their march toward doom. This time neither Wetzel nor Vanja could stop them.

At least Wizard was still holding out. Maybe he could do something.

Then Wizard walked forward, coming to join them. He too had been overwhelmed.

They were lost. Unless they could find some way to balk the monster before they reached it.

Wetzel got an idea. It was far-fetched, but it was all his struggling mind could produce at the moment.

He transformed back to manform. He found he could do that, because it wasn't resisting the deadly pull on his mind. The predator evidently didn't care what form its victims had, so long as they yielded to its imperative summons. Now he could talk.

"Veee!" he said.

She was right beside him. "Yes." She too could respond as long as she did not resist the monster.

"Hide from it," he said urgently. "Go to your storm shelter. It can't reach you there."

She nodded. Then she stopped walking. She had retreated into her secret place, and was no longer subject to the control of the monster.

But in a moment she resumed walking. "It worked," she said. "But I can't desert the rest of you."

"I can retreat similarly," Wetzel said.

"But that won't save the others."

And that was the problem. Saving just the two of them was not enough.

"Maybe Tod can help," she said. "Tod!"

Tod turned his head toward her without halting his marching. "Yes." He too could respond when specifically addressed.

"Wetzel and I can retreat inside ourselves and avoid the mind signal. But that won't help the rest of you. What can we do?"

"Like dogs. One distracts while the other attacks. Take turns distracting it while the other acts."

It was more complicated than that, but Wetzel got the picture from Tod's mind. "Do it!" he told her. "Make faces at the monster, or something. Tease it. Then retreat so it can't find you. Maybe then it won't be watching me."

She caught on immediately. "Hey, monster!" she exclaimed. "Sourpuss! Look at me! I'm escaping you!" And she stopped walking.

The grip on Wetzel's mind eased as the monster oriented on Veee. Wetzel strode to where Tod walked, put his arms around the man, and picked him up. He turned and strode back up the hill, carrying Tod. "That's the way," Tod said. "I wish I could help."

"You already helped, giving us the strategy."

Then the monster reoriented, and Wetzel lost control. He started turning around.

Now it was his turn. "Go jump in a lake of manure!" he said. "You can't hold me!" And he retreated into his own storm shelter.

He waited, uncertain whether Veee had emerged from her shelter yet, or how she was coping. He couldn't wait too long, lest the others be hauled on down.

He emerged and looked around. Veee was carrying Vanja up the slope. She had done it!

Then she stopped and began to turn back. "Nyaa Nyaa! You can't catch mee!" And went still.

The monster was distracted again. This was working! Wetzel still had Tod over his shoulder. He marched a few steps back, until the power grabbed his mind again. But he could still talk. "Vanja! Change to bat form so it's easier to carry you out."

He saw her change. Then he teased the monster again as he retreated.

When he came out of it, he found that Veee, freed of the weight of Vanja's body, had gone after Wizard and hauled him back a few steps. They were making progress.

But the monster was catching on. Next time Wetzel came out of hiding, the monster clamped down on his mind immediately, and he started carrying Tod back down the slope. Veee similarly paused, then marched down. The surprise was gone and the monster had resumed command.

"Act together," Tod said.

Wetzel tuned into Veee's mind, and when she retreated into her shelter, so did he. Then they emerged together, and started back up the slope before the monster could get both under control simultaneously.

Wetzel carried Tod several steps, and Veee carried Wizard, while the bat perched on Veee. They were making progress.

Until the monster adjusted to this new ploy and clamped down on them both. They turned about again and started tramping downhill. They were out of ploys, and losing.

Veee glanced at him. It seemed she could not speak except in response, and had something on her mind. Wetzel read her mind, and there it was. *The rape repellant*.

He realized that this would indeed be a better defense than mere hiding. The mind monster's attack was similar to a rape, and should be similarly balked. "Do it!" he said.

Veee focused. The awful repulsion surged. She had improved on it since he taught her. Copulation was disgusting, humiliating, and dirty. She was totally without sexual appeal.

But still walking toward the monster.

"Change it," he said. "The monster doesn't want sex, it wants flesh to eat. Make yourself repulsive as food."

She nodded. Her mental imagery shifted from an ugly genital region to a diseased body. She became a virtual zombie, walking decaying flesh, complete with maggots wriggling in holes in her skin. It was sickening. Wetzel almost smelled the stench.

Something changed.

"I'm free!" she exclaimed.

"Carry Wizard away," Wetzel told her. "When he is beyond range, return to carry another."

She hesitated. "I don't want to leave the rest of you in danger."

"Do it!" Tod snapped.

Veee hastily obeyed. She might be her own woman, but she was highly responsive to Tod.

Wetzel addressed the bat. "You were there when she learned rape repulsion. You know how it works. Do it."

The bat became the woman. "Do it yourself," she said, and started concentrating. The image of vomit suffused her mind.

She was right. Wetzel had been so busy addressing others he had neglected to see to himself. He had never been concerned about getting raped, knowing that even if someone wanted to do it to him, he could become the unicorn and destroy the rapist. Now he marshaled his feelings in earnest. He borrowed from Veee's imagery, making himself another zombie, and added open sores that leaked corrosive ichor.

And he was free. Just like that, they had found the way to stop the predator. It was repelled by bad meat. It seemed to be an automatic response.

"You can do it too," he told Tod. "Picture yourself as dirty, ugly, diseased, and foul-tasting. Maybe even poisonous. Something no self-respecting predator would eat."

Tod worked on it. It seemed he had once discovered a rotting carcass, and the odor had been appalling. He pictured himself as that noisome mass, complete with protruding bones.

It worked for him too. The three of them strode back up the slope, away from the predator.

They rejoined Veee and Wizard some distance back on the trail. "It seems we have had our first test as a reconstituted team," Wizard said. "One thing bothers me: why was I so incompetent? I should have devised magic to repel, confuse, or destroy the monster. Instead I was helpless."

"I can tell you why," Veee said. "The Amoeba is breaking in our new member. It put us on a route that passes a mental threat, rather than a magical one, so you could not handle it but Wetzel could, once he figured out how."

"You were the one who figured it out," Wetzel said. "You remembered the rape repellant. That was the key."

"Which you taught me," Veee said. "Then you figured out how to adapt it for this purpose."

Wetzel smiled. "You seem determined to give me credit I don't deserve."

"She does that," Wizard said. "She derives the rules of the game, then encourages others to play it. She doesn't seek credit herself. It is one of her endearing qualities. But she is right: it was your insight and technique that foiled the monster. Had we encountered it without you, we could have been lost."

"Had we been with someone else, the Amoeba would have led us past a different trap," Tod said.

"Next question," Vanja said. "What do we do about that monster? We can't let it go on eating innocent travelers."

"Now that we have nullified its power," Tod said, "we can attack it and destroy it. Wizard can fashion a magic bomb to blow it apart."

"I like that," Vanja said. "Maybe I can fly into its lair as a bat and spike it with a quick bite to the ugly snout, then change to human form and drain it dry."

"Two problems," Tod said. "It is probably too big to drain that way; you'd swell up and burst and be no further good to us. And its blood probably tastes like rotten swill."

"I could open a vein and let it bleed out on the ground."

"No," Veee said.

Vanja looked at her. "It was going to eat you! You can't forgive that."

"There's nothing to forgive," Veee said. "It's not a matter of right and wrong. It's a predator like any other. We just need to protect ourselves from it and its kind."

"Its kind," Vanja repeated thoughtfully.

"She's right again," Wizard said. "Predators don't grow in isolation any more than prey creatures do. There are ratios, overall balance, natural selection. There will be others like it, some with variants we have not yet thought of. It is the unknown ones ahead of us we need to anticipate and foil, not the one we have escaped. That is our lesson of the occasion."

"But it tried to consume all of us," Vanja protested. "I hate to let it go."

"Just as that rabbit you tapped hated to let you go," Veee said. "It would have smashed you if it could."

Vanja raised her hands in surrender. "I guess I'm just a bad sport about being considered prey. So let's devise our defense against future mental predators."

"I think we all need the three things Wetzel taught me," Veee said. "To recognize a mental touch before it becomes compulsive. To develop a rape or consumption repellant. To hide our most secret thoughts, so we can plan programs without giving them away, even to telepaths." She glanced at Wizard. "And to find ways to adapt magic to our defense too, in case some mental predator is proof against our other wiles."

"We had better do it now," Tod agreed. "We have had our warning. We can even test techniques on the local predator, to be sure they are effective."

"So the damn thing is useful after all," Vanja said distastefully.

They camped where they were and got to work. Wetzel drilled them all on recognition of the mind touch. They already knew how to prevent rape or consumption, thanks to their recent experience. It was the storm shelter that required more attention.

"You will not enjoy this," Wetzel said. "You need to revisit your deepest secret fear or shame, the one you most want to bury. That will be the basis for your construction of your personal retreat, your storm shelter. You could do this yourselves, as I did when I made mine, but it will be faster if I guide you."

"So you will know our most secret shames," Vanja said.

"Yes. I understand why you would not want to do that."

"So we'll start with you," Vanja said. "What's your secret?"

"As a young child I sneaked into a haunted house with a girl. We were playing Show-Me, and she stripped to her panties. Then the adults caught us, and the girl disappeared. I thought she had been punished for being willing to show herself, and I was frightened and ashamed. She was precociously telepathic; I suspected that this also could be the reason she was sequestered. But at the time I didn't know. Then when I also became precociously telepathic I feared I would be taken away and perhaps killed, so I found a way to hide. My storm shelter is the cellar where we played our naughty game. So my secret was that I had a secret. As an adult I know that it's not much of a crime, but it did enable me to make my shelter."

"You're right," Vanja said. "We don't care at all about any such guilt. Every boy wants to look at every girl nude. Every girl secretly wants to show it off." Her clothing faded momentarily to nudity. "Who's next?"

"I will do it," Wizard said. "My secret is truly guilty, because it derives from an episode when I was adult and knew better. The giantess who governed our region was a beautiful woman, when she tried to be, and she sought to seduce me and thus bind me to her. I resisted, of course; I was in a long-term happy marriage. But once when I was scrying for her she quietly stripped, stepped into me, kissed me, and seduced me. I fought against it, but her sheer eroticism overwhelmed me."

"We saw her," Vanja said. "She was like me: lovely, wild, and unscrupulous."

"We did see her," Tod agreed. There was a mental flash of a remarkably sexy nude woman in motion.

"She mesmerized you," Veee said fondly. "You couldn't stop staring at her bare body."

"She was standing right over me, fifty feet tall, her legs spread," Tod said reminiscently. "Then these two jealous females hauled me out of there."

"You were freaking out, you letch," Vanja said.

Wetzel saw the enhanced image in Tod's mind. "I would have freaked out too," he said. "What a view!"

"So we don't blame you for falling under her spell, Wiz," Vanja said.

"Thereafter I guarded myself with magic," Wizard said, returning to the subject. "Not the neat repulsion mind-frame we have recently learned, merely a field that made me difficult to approach close enough for sex. I was on guard, and it never happened again. But I knew my wife would not understand, and I hid it from her. Thus my infidelity was compounded by the lie that was my concealment. It remains my deepest shame."

"That will do," Tod said. "Fashion a chamber around that memory. Encapsulate it. Then when you have a secret to hide, bring it into that chamber and leave it there. It may take time to perfect the technique, but if you practice you will improve, until there is no evidence of your shelter, even to telepaths."

"I will," Wizard said.

"I think it is my turn next," Tod said.

There was a gust of wind. Veee looked at the sky. "Storm. It may be a bad one."

Vanja changed to bat form and flew up. The wind caught her and blew her to the side. She landed and changed. "Bad one," she agreed. "We haven't seen weather like this before. Not in the amoeba. It's just one thing after another."

"I suspect the Amoeba," Wizard said. "It is putting us through a course, forcing us to develop techniques we may need for the mission."

"For a thing that takes no direct action, it's pretty active," Tod said sourly.

"It is merely a particular trail, one with challenges," Wizard said. "We need to organize in key ways before the crisis comes."

"Well, right now we're in danger of getting blown away," Vanja said. "We need to find shelter, and there's nothing I've seen from the air."

"I will scry," Wizard said. "I am better with subjects I can touch, but I am touching the air and can fathom it to an extent."

"We know there's a storm," Veee said. "Scry the ground for shelter."

"Good thought." Wizard put a hand down on the ground. "Oh, my."

"Don't get cute, Wiz," Vanja said. "What's the answer?"

"You won't like this."

"I'm not a child! Out with it."

"The only suitable cave within range is that of the mind monster."

Vanja stepped back as if struck. "You're right. I don't like it."

"We escaped it," Tod said. "Now we have to join it? That's risky."

"Less risky than the coming storm," Wizard said. "It's a cyclone."

"A hurricane?" Tod was plainly impressed. "We do need to get under cover."

"We have learned how to turn off the monster's appetite,"

Veee said. "We should be able to approach it if we do so in a non-threatening manner, so it doesn't have to defend itself."

"Oh, joy," Vanja muttered.

Tod turned to Wizard. "If we go there, and the thing has a change of appetite, can you bomb it?"

"I can," Wizard agreed.

"Don't do that unless you have to," Veee said.

There was another gust of wind, this one stronger, carrying leaves and twigs. The storm was incipient.

"Let's go," Tod said. They reformed their formation and moved out, this time maintaining their don't-eat moods.

The trip was rapid, now that they weren't fighting anything. Soon they reached the base of the hill beyond their prior struggle, and followed the path to a bank. There was the cave entrance.

And there too was the monster. "A giant hermit crab," Tod said. "Or maybe an ant lion, on a larger scale." The images in his mind seemed apt. The thing seemed to be as large as a unicorn. Those pincers looked quite capable of severing limbs.

"Do we have to?" Vanja asked plaintively.

Another blast of wind whipped her black hair to the side as if trying to tear it out. More debris flew by. A nearby tree leaned dangerously. That was answer enough.

Wizard dismounted, and Wetzel resumed manform. He quested for the crab's mind. "We have become non-prey to it," he said.

"Its body blocks the whole cave entrance," Tod said.

"So the cave is tight against the storm," Wizard said. "We simply need to persuade it to let us pass."

"To squeeze by it?" Vanja asked. "I'd rather drink bad blood and puke."

"Check its mind, Wetzel," Tod said. "Find out how we can deal with it."

Wetzel checked. "It doesn't care about us now, since we dropped off the prey list. All it's thinking of is a really sore muscle it got from cracking open too hard a bone a few days ago."

"The poor thing!" Vanja said witheringly.

"Maybe we can deal," Veee said. "If we fix the muscle, it may let us through."

"Maybe if we plug it through the head, it will die and let us through," Vanja said.

"We can't make any deal if we can't communicate," Tod pointed out.

"Ah, but we can," Wizard said. "The creature is at least semi-telepathic. That's how it summons its prey. We just need to think the right thought."

"A thought of healing and relief of pain," Veee said. "Associated with a thought of sharing its cave with a party of five inedibles."

"That thought would be a promise," Tod said. "But we would need to deliver."

"How?" Vanja asked sharply.

Veee looked at her.

"Oh, no! I'm not helping that brute any way short of killing it."

"We need you, Vamp," Wizard said. "Are you up to the sacrifice?"

Another storm gust almost blew them off their feet. "Oh, for Pedro's sake!" Vanja formed a mood of healing, especially of a painful muscle, buttressed by the thought of sharing. She advanced on the crab. "Show me where it hurts, Crabby." Her mind pictured a muscle radiating pain.

The crab extended a giant pincer. At its base was a reddish area. "That's it," Wetzel said.

Vanja stepped close and put her fang to it. She bit, slowly, paused a moment, then carefully withdrew.

"The pain is fading," Wetzel reported.

"Of course it is," Vanja said. "I injected anesthetic. It won't cure it, but it will relax it so it can heal."

"So we have delivered our favor," Tod said. "Will it reciprocate?"

"Let me try," Wetzel said. "I will know its intention in time to escape if I have to." He walked to the crab.

The crab retreated into its hole, making room to pass. Wetzel squeezed by it, and walked on into the dark cave. It stank of crab dung, but was otherwise habitable.

The others followed, as the wind tore at them with increasing fervor. Soon they were all inside.

"What a stench!" Vanja complained. "I'll take bat guano over this anytime."

"Fortunately there are vents," Veee said, putting her face by a crevice that let in a wan gleam of light and some fresh air. "Here's another, Vanja."

Vanja joined her, inhaling the slip of fresh air.

The tempest intensified, now carrying rain and hailstones. The crab moved forward, blocking the entry, and the weather receded. They were safe from the storm.

"Isn't this better?" Veee asked Vanja.

"Very well, you distaff canine!" the vampire snapped. "It is marginally better than getting blown away."

Veee kissed her.

"Now, while we are waiting," Wizard said, "You may resume your narration, Tod, and fashion your storm shelter. There is hardly a more fitting place to do it than this."

Tod laughed. "Indeed, it is appropriate. My most secret shame is from childhood. We had something to go to, I no longer remember what, maybe the library, and I was asked whether I needed to use the toilet before I went. I said I didn't. Then I was caught by an urgent need and pooped my pants. I was so embarrassed that I sneaked into the facility restroom and cleaned up and washed out my shorts myself, wrung them out and put them back on damp. I never told anyone, always fearing that somehow it would be discovered, but it never was. So it remains my secret, until now."

"That library," Wetzel said. "That could be your shelter."

They worked at it, and gradually Tod got it. He had his shelter.

Then it was Vanja's turn. "Yours was poop," she said. "Mine was similar. As a child once I was in a group event with several other girls, and my digestion turned on me. I got horrible gas. I managed to let it out silently, but it was a heroically worthy stink, worse than what's here in this cave. Naturally the other girls soon smelled it, and made exaggerated choking and retching sounds before guessing who was responsible. They finally pinned it on another girl, who of course denied it, but they called her a liar and she was stuck with it." Vanja took a breath. "I was silent, letting her take the blame. She was my friend. That's my shame: that I did that to my friend. I swore never to do that again."

"So the experience made you a more honest person," Wizard said. "Now that is part of what we respect in you."

"I still hate the thought," Vanja said. Then she worked on it, and in due course had her storm shelter.

Then all they had to do was wait out the storm. They stood by their vents, breathing the turbulent drafts, and slept standing. When they needed to, they added to the refuse of the cave. Fortunately it was large enough to hold any amount, and the older material was composting.

Their primary enemy became boredom. "Let's practice our arts," Veee said. "Tell us a diverting story, Wizard."

They had arts? Wetzel hadn't realized. He had his own interest in Drama; would that mesh?

"Once upon a time there was a virgin in search of a unicorn," Wizard said.

"I'll be the virgin," Vanja said. "That requires an extraordinary feat of acting. I will do a Virgin Dance to summon that handsome beast. Set the stage, Veee."

"A cave in a forest, shelter from a storm," Veee said.

Vanja accepted that. "Music, maestro."

Tod got out a small musical instrument, an ocarina, and played a flute-like melody. It was surprisingly good; it was lovely music. Vanja danced to it, and in the gloom her body almost seemed to glow.

Wetzel, of course, was the unicorn. There was room in the cave; he transformed and allowed himself to be enchanted by the Virgin.

The story continued from there, involving the other team members; everyone had a part to play. Wizard had a talent for narration, and it was a fair diversion. The interim became almost pleasant despite the ugly setting. They were all pleased. Their several talents helped them to get along well. Even the crab monster seemed to be tuning in in its fashion.

Next morning, by Tod's timepiece, the storm was abating. They broached the crab, who obligingly let them out. Vanja paused to give it another bite, extending the pain relief.

"There may be no redemption for your shame," Wetzel said. "But what you have done for a creature you regard as your enemy might be a kind of redemption."

"It's what Veee would do," Vanja said simply. "She wanted to spare this creature."

"It taught us the need for storm shelters," Veee said. "And how to avoid a dangerous summons.

They looked around. The local landscape was a wreckage. Many trees had been blown down, and much of the underbrush had been scoured away. They had to pick their way through; the path no longer existed.

"I'll scout the best route." Vanja changed and flew up. In a moment Wetzel caught her mental image: there were more wolfkeys prowling. They were scooting around and under the fallen wood, heading this way.

"Wolfkeys," Wetzel said.

"We're at a disadvantage in this wreckage," Tod said. "They can hide and pounce from ambush."

"No," Wetzel said. "I can read their minds." Then he reconsidered. "Their minds are locked. They're not stalking us."

"The crab!" Wizard said. "They came within range, and it caught them."

They stood and watched as the first wolfkey emerged from under a trunk and walked toward the crab. The crab's pincers caught it and cut it into pieces. Then the crab's mouth crunched the pieces.

"It eats wolfkeys!" Vanja breathed. "Now I know why we spared it!"

"I thought it might have its uses," Veee said.

"And here I thought you were just softhearted."

"That, too," Veee agreed, smiling.

"It surely helps keep down their numbers," Tod agreed. "That pack won't be following us beyond this point."

They resumed their advance, no longer concerned about predators. Wetzel wondered when they would discover their mission. If this was all merely preparation for it, it could be some challenge.

CHAPTER 5: MISSION

———

They picked their way back up the hill to the trail. This was miraculously undamaged.

Miraculously? Wetzel realized that the Amoeba was a creature of trails, so must safeguard them. They might have been safe if they had simply hunkered down on the trail and let the storm pass. Might have. He was hardly sure enough of that to risk it if another storm came. The wolfkeys had attacked them on the trail, after all, so it was not safe in that sense.

They made good progress, and in the early afternoon came to another village. "Caution," Wizard advised. "Chances are they will ignore us, recognizing us as being on Amoeba business. But we should not assume too much. They might possibly be hostile."

But as they approached it, a person came out to meet them. "Welcome, travelers!" he called. He was a handsome man of middle age with brick-red hair and beard. "We have been expecting you."

His mind indicted just such an expectation.

"Expecting us?" Tod asked. "We expected just to pass through, on our way to our mission."

"Your mission is here," the man said. "I am Red, mayor of RedBrick Village." He smiled. "Because of my hair, you know; it matches. Whoever is closest in color is mayor. And you are?"

"I am Tod," Tod said.

"Come, Tod, and party; we have reserved facilities for you." Red glanced at Wetzel. "Though I admit we had not anticipated a unicorn or a bat. Will a stall do?"

"Before we proceed further," Tod said quickly, "we need to be sure there is not some confusion. What mission are you thinking of?"

"Beetle Juice, of course," Red said.

Those were the key words. "Then we shall gratefully accept your hospitality," Tod said. "This is Veee, and Wizard. The unicorn and bat are also members of our party."

Wetzel appreciated Tod's caution. The villagers could have heard the words and recognized them as an Amoeba project, and set up to waylay the team when it appeared. Like wolfkeys or the telepathic hermit crab. So Tod was accepting the offer, but remaining on guard. Neither Wetzel nor Vanja made any sign.

"We may have a problem," Red said. "Bats eat bugs."

"They do," Tod agreed. "What is the problem?"

"This is complicated, and you will need a thorough briefing. But the essence is that we are trying to preserve a vitally important beetle, which we call the scarab, and we dare not risk it getting eaten."

This did not sound like a trap. "Vanja," Tod said.

Vanja jumped off Wetzel's head, transformed in mid air, and landed neatly on her feet, her scantily clad flesh bouncing. Red's eyes were locked onto each bounce, exactly as she intended. "I am a bat, but not only a bat," she said. "I am a vampire."

Red was visibly relieved. "Suck all the blood you want, you luscious creature," he said. "Just don't eat the scarab."

Meanwhile Tod caught Wetzel's eye, silently querying him. Wetzel was ready. Red's mind showed no subterfuge, no animosity, no trap. He was legitimate, and he did have a very serious concern with a beetle of some sort. It was not exactly a scarab, except in the sense that it was immensely valuable. In Tod's mind was the information that scarabs had been regarded as sacred by an ancient culture.

Wizard dismounted, and Wetzel converted to manform. Veee immediately tossed him undershorts, and he donned them as he spoke. "And I am Wetzel, a were-unicorn." He did not mention telepathy; that seemed best omitted. "I will not need a stall."

Red smiled. "The Amoeba is handling this in style. This way, please." He turned, offering his arm to Vanja, who took it. Tod and Veee followed, satisfied to become background, and Wetzel and Wizard followed them.

The village consisted of red brick houses with red thatched roofs. A number of men were there, going about their business, not paying overt attention to the visiting party. But their minds were attuned; they we eager for the mission to proceed. The mission of saving the beetle.

Wetzel knew the other members of the team were as perplexed as he was, because he read their minds. Their job, after all this preparation, was to save a bug?

Their house was spacious and clean, with kitchen facilities and beds for five. It had running water and a picture window. This was not a primitive village.

"Settle in, get rested," Red told them. "This evening I will brief you on the situation. We certainly hope you can help us."

"We hope so too," Tod said.

"We will certainly try," Vanja said, kissing Red on the cheek. Wetzel felt the impact on the man's mind; Red was hungry for the favor of any woman, especially a beautiful one. Red departed, still feeling that kiss.

"This village has no women," Veee said.

"I noticed," Vanja said. "I could have seduced that man without even trying. Maybe I will, tonight."

"There are no women," Wetzel agreed. "Yet they are heterosexual men who crave female companionship. That is as far as I have been able to read, so far."

"We can inquire during the briefing," Wizard said. "Wetzel will get an answer even if they try to avoid it."

They used the facilities, cleaning up and relaxing. "During the briefing," Wizard said, "I believe we should be open minded but not demonstrate any more abilities than we have already." He glanced at Wetzel.

Wetzel nodded. He would keep the telepathy secret. It was not something the villagers needed to know, and it was bound to be useful.

There was a knock on the door. A young man stood there, bearing a large covered platter. "Your dinner, if you please," he said.

"Thank you," Veee said, accepting it.

The man stood there, fidgeting.

Vanja approached him. "There is something more?"

"When—when Red brought you here, you—you kissed him."

"Oh." She leaned forward and kissed him on the cheek.

He departed, dazed.

"They really, really need women here," Vanja remarked.

"They seem well enough off," Tod said. "Surely they could attract women, if they tried."

"They aren't trying," Wetzel said. "There's some reason they don't want women here, and it's not because they don't like them. I can't read any deeper, so far."

"I really must seduce the mayor, and get the truth," Vanja said. She glanced at Wetzel. "Don't worry; I'll seduce you too, later."

Wetzel smiled. She was serious, and he had to agree with her: whatever information he couldn't get telepathically, she could probably get personally.

The food was excellent: bread, wine, eggs, vegetables, and pudding for dessert. There were five portions, accounting for all of them.

When they had eaten, the young man came again to remove the dishes. Vanja kissed him again, thrilling him again. "As payment goes, this is minimal," she said.

Red returned. He settled himself on a chair and addressed them all. "Here is the situation: this is the neighborhood of the scarab, perhaps the rarest and most important beetle known. Here is a picture rendered by one of our artists." He held up a painting.

"I'll be damned!" Tod said. "That's the Mandlebrot set!"

"The what?" Red asked.

"One of the most complicated and beautiful designs known," Tod said. "It is derived mathematically. I'm not clear on the exact process, but I understand it is the plotting of a complex number geometrically. The border between the dark center and the light background takes the general form of a hairy bug, but it is vastly more than that. I used to get lost contemplating its detail pictures. The greater the magnification, the more complicated the pattern, seemingly without end. Every curlicue of its detail is anchored by a miniature bug like the original one, only much smaller. And that miniature bug has its own curlicues, ever more elaborate until the eye and mind boggle with the sheer wonder of it. That is this picture."

"I don't know anything about all that," Red said. "This is a picture of a living scarab that is incalculably precious. Its dead husk is used for jewelry. A live one is squished for its juice, which promotes human health and longevity. Some even say immortality. That's its real commercial value. That's why poachers steal it and sell it, becoming fabulously wealthy. That's why it is in imminent danger of extinction. When it is lost, the universe will be a worse place. We have to save it. That's why we prayed to the Amoeba, and why the Amoeba has answered with your team. Your mission is to save the beetle."

Wetzel was aware of Tod's annoyance as his insight was sloughed off, but the man gave no outward sign. Wizard was similarly annoyed and similarly suppressed. Veee was intrigued by both Tod's description of the design and Red's description of the plight of the scarab. She was interested in art of any type and the mere suggestion of this complicated geometric set fascinated her, but she also had empathy for all living things. She would be the mediator.

"Of course we must save the scarab," Veee agreed warmly. "Tell us more about it."

Wetzel picked up how Red warmed to her. Naturally Vanja had impressed him initially, but Veee was female too, and not unattractive when allowance was made for her size and muscle. She could affect a man when she tried.

"The scarab is prettier than any picture can show," Red said. "It scintillates with colors that go beyond what the eye can see. To gaze at it is to love it. But the predation has been so severe that now we seldom see one."

"They have learned to hide," Veee said.

"We hope so. Otherwise they are doomed."

"I am not clear how we can save a beetle we can't find," Tod said.

"It must be possible, or the Amoeba would not have sent you."

"Maybe it is saving itself by hiding," Veee said.

"Yet that will not be enough," Red said. "If they could remain hidden all the time, maybe then it would work. But they can't."

"Why not?" Veee asked gently, somehow making it seem like support rather than challenge.

"They are a dual-habitat creature." Then, seeing their blankness, Red explained. "They have a complicated life cycle, and can reproduce only in the normal universe, on a planet orbiting a star in the vicinity of Betelgeuse. Then they enter the Amoeba and mature. RedBrick Village is by the gateway: the trail that connects the scarab's world to the Amoeba. They are safe here, but not on their home world, which is where the poachers trap them. If they could reproduce here they could be saved, but they can't."

"There is no law forbidding poaching?" Tod asked.

"It's an unsettled planet, set aside as a scarab preserve. Intrusion is forbidden. But the poachers know no law. They sneak in, catch the beetles, and escape before the authorities can stop them. They are well armed, so that when they are caught, they simply blast apart the ranger's ships and escape anyway."

"We have poachers like that in my frame," Tod said. "They go after rare wild animals, and they kill anyone who tries to stop them."

"Exactly," Red agreed. "The planet is too big to police completely. Many poachers are caught and killed, but the scarab is so valuable that there are always more, just as vicious. I'd like to kill them all, but that's hopeless. As long as the scarab exists, there will be poachers. Too many people are desperate for the health and longevity the beetle juice provides. The beetles live a long time; they may even be immortal, as we have never heard of one dying naturally. But the poachers kill them."

"How did they come here?" Veee asked.

"The Amoeba brought them in, to save them, centuries ago. We maintain the local habitat so that it is ideal for them. But it's not enough."

"I am not clear why they can reproduce only on their home world, if the Amoeba's habitat is ideal," Wizard said.

"They are mostly females," Red said. "We believe that males are rarely hatched, maybe only once a century, and that occurs only on the home world. We've never seen a male, but it must be spectacular."

"Indeed," Veee agreed warmly.

"There is one other thing," Red said. "We suspect they are telepathic. That's how they know to avoid people."

None of the team gave any sign, but all were electrified by the news. Now it was clear why Wetzel had been summoned.

"We will see what we can do," Tod said. "We'll think about the problem."

"This is not a time for thinking," Red said sharply. "It's the time for action."

"We must consider ways and means," Wizard said. "At this point we don't know what is appropriate. Inappropriate action would be worse than no action."

"We are sure you understand," Veee said. "We do very much value your help."

Red thawed somewhat. "Yes, of course."

"Meanwhile you can explain why there are no women in your village," Vanja said, flashing him with her flexible décolletage. "Healthy men like you should have women flocking."

"It is not entirely by choice," Red said, properly mesmerized by that décolletage. "The local colony is all female, and they don't seem to understand about things like, well, mating. They pick up our emotions and are repelled. So to make it possible to approach the scarabs, we have to eschew any such relations. We can indulge in them only well away from the local preserve. Thus we have segregated villages, all male and all female." He took a heavy breath. "It's hell. Worse, we do not get along with our closest female neighbor, who guards the access to the scarab's home turf. There have been unfortunate episodes."

Wetzel picked up on it. Stray women caught by the desperately sex-hungry men had been tied, bug-sprayed, and gang raped. The women had reciprocated in kind tying men to trees and making them service women for food or to avoid torture. Use it or lose it was literal. So they got sex, but not love. There were some "dates" where individual men and women made deals and met beyond the beetles' range to indulge, but these were fraught with complications.

"So I can't go with you and make you deliriously happy for a few minutes," Vanja said. "It would repel the bugs."

"That is true," Red said, tearing his gaze away. "I will leave you to your considerations." He departed.

Tod turned immediately to Wetzel. "What did you get?"

"He's telling the truth. The local villages are strictly same-sex and they don't like it but have to do it. When a man can't stand it any longer, he departs and resumes normal heterosexual activity far away."

"Why do they stay even briefly?" Vanja asked.

"They are very well paid in coins and goods," Wetzel said. "And it is an honor to serve here."

"But if the beetle goes extinct, they will have no job," Tod said.

"So they have incentive, apart from being dedicated to the welfare of the beetle," Wizard said.

"They have incentive," Wetzel agreed. "They truly want to save the scarab."

"Then it behooves us to facilitate their effort," Wizard said. "The question is, how?"

"I have a more immediate one," Vanja said. "How can I make out with Wetzel, or Tod with Veee, here in the village?"

They considered that, not pleased.

"Do we have to honor the rules of the village?" Tod asked.

"We should," Wizard said. "Apart from the fact that we do want to be able to get close enough to the scarabs to be able to do them some good."

"I'll go crazy," Vanja said.

Wizard smiled. "I understood that was your normal state."

"Ha. Ha. Ha. How do we really know the bugs can't tolerate sex? That's just the opinion of the villagers. Besides which, if the bugs are near extinction there may not be any around here close enough anyway."

Wetzel got up and went silently to Tod. "Something else," he murmured in the man's ear so that only he could hear. "They have something they call a radio planted here, but I don't think it grows."

A radio bug! Tod thought immediately. *A little machine, a device to listen to what is said, and send it to a receiver elsewhere in the village, so they know what we say."*

"Also a silent alarm on the door," Wetzel murmured.

So they know if we try to leave. They don't trust us at all.

Wetzel returned to his place, knowing that Tod would handle the information as he saw fit. The others did not comment or give any sign, knowing Wetzel had picked up on something.

Tod beckoned Veee. When she came to him, he sat her on his lap and kissed her ear, whispering. Her eyes widened and her mouth thinned. She was annoyed.

After Veee, Tod whispered similarly to Vanja. She nodded, then went to whisper to Wizard, who seemed neither surprised nor annoyed. He might have scried the same information.

Now they all knew to watch their words, at least while they were in this village. They also knew how the stricture against sex was enforced; they would be banished from the village if they ignored that prohibition. The telepathy was paying off again.

"Let's compromise," Tod said. "No sex tonight. Tomorrow we will reconsider. We might be back on the trail by then."

The others nodded, reluctantly agreeing.

When night fell, Tod quietly went to the door and inspected it closely. *There's the alarm trigger*, he thought for Wetzel's benefit. *It's a simple one. I am deactivating it.*

So they could leave privately if they had to. Meanwhile the others were searching the house. Veee found the bug, a small device with wires fastened under the table, not normally in view. That one they left alone, as there would be immediate suspicion if it stopped sending.

They used the five beds, separately. Wetzel had, in the brief time he had been with the team, gotten used to Vanja's considerable nocturnal attentions, and he knew that Tod and Veee both liked theirs. It was surprising how frustrating it was to be celibate in practice as well as technically.

Wetzel, Vanja thought in the middle of the night. *If you read this, you're as restless as I am. Meet me outside.*

He did read it. He got up quietly and went outside, checking mentally for villagers. There were none awake. Only Vanja, in completely dark garb so that she was almost invisible in the night.

Change, Vanja thought from beside him.

He transformed to unicorn form. She went to bat form, flew

up and perched on his head. *Get far enough away to be beyond the beetles' range.*

He walked quietly out of the village, then when the sound of his hooves would not carry back that far he trotted farther, then galloped along the trail back the way they had come to the village. Soon Vanja reverted to human form and rode his back, mentally dwelling on the way her hot thighs were spread wide and her crotch bouncing on his backbone. *Yes, I'm firing you up.* She was correct; her thighs and her mind were having potent effect.

When the distance seemed sufficient he halted, breathing pleasantly hard. It was not completely dark here; there seemed to be a faint general glow from the foliage. Vanja dismounted, her apparent clothing fading to complete nudity. She pirouetted, arms lifted, showing off her complete figure. He appreciated it exactly as intended.

Wordlessly they embraced. She kissed him, her sheer need further inflaming his desire. She hung on tightly, lifted her legs, wrapped them around his waist, and maneuvered until his erect member found the entry. He thrust in, ejaculating explosively as her channel rhythmically squeezed with her own climax. Their mutual orgasm seemed to fill the universe, like a star going nova.

They remained in place as it faded, just appreciating the fulfillment. They were not in love, but understood each other, and their interest in sex was parallel. He needed the release; she needed the semen. They shared their bliss.

Then they changed again, and the bat rode the unicorn back toward the village of RedBrick. They had never spoken aloud.

No villagers were close. They reverted to human forms and quietly entered the house, returning to their separate beds.

Was it good? Veee's thought came.

He chuckled. "Yes," he murmured, knowing the radio bug would not understand what he was responding to.

If we're here tomorrow night, my turn with Tod.

"Yes," he repeated, smiling. Then he slept, no longer restless.

In the morning Tod carefully reactivated the silent alarm on the door, and addressed them openly. "As yet I have no idea how to proceed with the scarab. I think we need to get more of the larger situation," he said. "That means talking to the women also. We can ask the men where their village is, and go there, hoping they will have useful information. Then we well have a better basis to fashion our campaign to save the scarab."

"Will they allow sex at the women's village?" Vanja asked.

"I doubt it. That village should be in the beetle's region, as is the men's village. You will simply have to endure a while longer."

"Guano!" Vanja muttered at the table. The others smiled.

The assistant brought them a fine breakfast, and was rewarded with another kiss on the cheek.

In due course Red knocked, maintaining the pretense of their privacy. "Have you formulated a plan?" he inquired, though he knew they had not.

"We want to visit the women's village and get their information," Tod said. "We are, frankly, at a loss at this stage. But we will not quit until we have accomplished our mission."

"That's good," Red said. "The neighboring women's village is PinkPebble, about half a day's walk along the trail. But I must warn you that they have the same restrictions we do, and will not be friendly if you violate their strictures."

"We understand," Tod said. "We will honor the rules of the house, as we do here."

If Red appreciated the irony of that statement, he gave no sign.

"We wish you early success."

They set off along the trail in the direction indicated, Wizard and the bat riding the unicorn, Tod and Veee walking. They paused only for lunch, using their packed supplies, and did not speak of telepathy or their impression of RedBrick Village, alert to the chance of some other radio bug being with them.

The women's village was, of course, fashioned of pink stone walls with yellow thatched roofs, and was femininely pretty. The mayor, alert for their arrival, came out to meet them. "Welcome, travelers!" she said. She was a well-endowed woman with, naturally, flouncing pink hair. "I am Pinkie, and you must be the team sent by the Amoeba to solve our problem."

"We may be," Tod said. "We visited RedBrick, and learned some things about the scarab, but thought we needed to get your information too."

"You certainly do," Pinkie said. "You can't trust anything those men said without verification."

Wizard dismounted, and Wetzel and Vanja transformed to human. Pinkie did not look surprised. Obviously she knew about them. "I am Tod. This is Veee, and Wizard. Wetzel is a were-unicorn, and Vanja is a vampire. We work together."

"Come this way." Pinkie turned to lead them into the village.

Wetzel was not the only one taken aback. There was a large spider in her hair. Then Wetzel knew from her mind that she knew this, and was not alarmed; indeed the spider was there by invitation. It kept her hair neat, and protected her from biting flies.

"We have one stricture you may already know about," Pinkie said as she walked. "You are a mixed group, but you must not have intimate relations here in the village."

"We do know about it," Tod said. "We will honor your stricture while we are here."

The house was if anything even nicer than the one in the other village. It was fully equipped, and its pantry was well stocked so that they could make their own meals. "I will give you time to get comfortable, then return to brief you," Pinkie said, departing.

They were somewhat dusty from their journey, so did avail themselves of the amenities. Vanja and Veee stripped and walked naked to the shower, giving the men a deliberate show. Then it was the men's turn, giving the girls a show. Wizard did not need to shower; he simply wove a spell of cleanliness, and the dust dissipated.

Before they could see about making dinner, there was a knock. There stood a stunningly lovely young woman with a beehive hairdo. Bees actually buzzed around it. "I am Pisa," she said. "I have come to invite you to the evening banquet."

"We shall be glad to attend," Tod said graciously. "But if I may ask—"

"We all have our hair tended by insects or arachnids," Pisa said. "We like them, and they are useful. My bees keep my hair orderly, and discourage any unkind attention."

"Thank you," Tod said.

She dipped her gaze demurely. "But they don't discourage kind attention. If you should be interested, I know a private place."

"I appreciate your interest," Tod said. "But I am otherwise committed."

Pisa turned to give him a marvelous peek inside her low décolletage. Wetzel picked it up from Tod's mind. "Are you sure?"

"I am sure," Tod said. The man had discipline.

"Perhaps another time," she said. Wetzel read her disappointment. She was desperately hungry not for romance, but for a baby.

Wizard, Veee, and Vanja all kept straight faces, intrigued and amused.

"This way, please," Pisa said, turning to display her remarkable silhouette. Obviously she had not given up hope.

Then Wetzel felt the feather touch of his mind. Instantly he buried any awareness of his telepathy. He glanced around, and saw that the others had felt the touch too. So all of them were on guard, protecting their secrets.

So there was a telepath in the vicinity. That was both interesting and challenging.

Pisa led them to a larger house with a banquet hall. The other women of the village had gathered and were standing at their places, all of them well dressed. Wetzel picked up the ambient mood: despite the stricture against sex, they remained interested in making a good impression. This was partly because they expected to work with the visiting team, partly because they liked the chance to be good hostesses, partly for the novelty of company, and partly because any and all of them were desperate for male company with all it implied. Pisa was not the exception but the rule.

Pinkie stood at the circular head table. "Please join me," she said formally. "Your places are marked."

Indeed they were, with neat little placards. Each member of the team was correctly named. The men alternated with the women, Pinkie herself part of it so that the pattern was complete. They were a table of six.

The food was served, and it was sumptuous, with all manner of meats, vegetables, breads, pastries, and beverages. It was evident that the women of PinkPebble liked to cook and bake.

Wetzel was not the only one aware of the hairdos of other women as they moved about. One resembled an anthill with red ants that surely would bite anyone who bothered her. Another was a wasp nest with a constant buzz of wasps coming and going. Another had scorpions. Others had dragonflies, butterflies, ladybugs, or termites. One even swarmed with tiny fruit flies. None harmed the women, and some were quite pretty.

"We do favor insects here," Pinkie said, observing their interest. "And of course spiders. Our fellow travelers protect us and serve us, not to mention keeping our hair neat and interesting. You will want to acquire similar friends yourselves."

"We will?" Tod asked, surprised.

"You will not be able to get close to the beetles unless you demonstrate some affinity for their kind. That is why we adopted the insects; it makes us compatible."

"How does a person adopt an insect?" Tod asked.

"Actually it is the other way around," Pinkie said. "The insects adopt the people. They are mildly telepathic, and know the true feelings of those they encounter. They will not befriend anyone who does not truly want it."

Wetzel remembered a stray reference he had read in Red's mind: bug-spraying captured women. It wasn't that they were unclean, but that they were protected by their bugs. A woman with hornets in her hair would not be readily raped unless the hornets were killed.

There were nasty aspects to this situation.

Now Wizard had a question. "As I understand it, it is the scarab we have to save, not any other insect. Why should we befriend non-beetles?"

"For the same reason we do," Pinkie answered. "To demonstrate that you are not hostile to any type of insect. You can't approach the scarab directly; you must win its confidence in stages."

"And if we win that confidence," Wizard asked, "How will that facilitate our mission?"

"I don't know. But you certainly can't help the scarab if you never get close to it."

Wizard nodded, accepting that.

"We will try to befriend the insects," Tod said. "Then we will consider the next stage."

The dinner finished, they cleared the tables and set the chairs around the edges of the chamber. "Now the dance," Pinkie said.

The younger women put on a phenomenal show, twirling in their flaring skirts, showing off their legs and just about everything else. It was highly seductive. Then they came after the five members of the team, dancing with them. It was easy to do; all they had to do was stand in the vicinity while several girls whirled around each, like orbiting planets, swooping in to steal quick kisses. The men obviously liked it; Veee and Vanja less so.

One of Wetzel's orbiters was Pisa, with the beehive. She had evidently given up on Tod and now was trying the next. Both her body and her mind were highly suggestive. "I know you are the unicorn," she murmured during a swoop. "And I am a virgin."

And she was! That paralyzed Wetzel, who had somehow not picked up on that before. Suddenly he had to have her.

She knew she had gotten to him. She took his hand and led him outside. The other girls did not protest; she was doing what any of them would have done, given the chance.

It was dusk. "Change," she said. "Let me ride you." Her mind was fully conscious of the double entente.

He doffed his clothing, bundled it, handed it to her, and transformed. She leaped onto his back. "Down that street," she said, pointing. "It leads directly out of the scarab region."

He galloped down the street. Soon it emerged from the village and cut straight through the forest. It led to an isolated house. "That's our love nest," Pisa said. "Girls make dates to meet men there."

They drew up at the house. Pisa dismounted, and Wetzel transformed back to manform. They entered.

Inside was a room with a bed. That was all. It was indeed intended for trysts.

Pisa almost ripped off her clothing. Wetzel was of course already naked.

She flung herself onto the bed, face up. "Do it!" she said, spreading her legs. Evidently she wasn't interested in foreplay.

He joined her, his erection manifest.

She took one look and screamed.

What?

"I can't do it!" she cried. "I thought I could, I wanted to, I want to get a baby, but I can't!"

It was the virgin syndrome. In his eagerness he had let it slip his mind: virgins were not eager for sex with him. They had to be wooed, cajoled, persuaded, seduced, and then it wasn't certain. The process normally took days or weeks. No such time was available here.

"Damn," he muttered, turning away.

"Wait!" Pisa cried. "I can't do it, but you can! Jump on me, hold me down, do it!"

"I can't do that. It's rape."

"But men do that all the time to women. Some of our villagers have been raped. I really want my baby. Make me have it."

"I can't," he repeated. "Neither morally nor physically. Because it would be wrong, and because I can't force any woman, let alone a virgin."

"But can't a virgin make you do anything she wants?"

"Yes. But you don't want this."

"Yes I do! My spirit is willing. It's my body that's weak. My bees know it. See, they're not angry." She was right; the bees were resting on and in the hive.

"You want a baby," Wetzel said. "You know you have to have sex to get it. But you don't want sex with me. You are not willing. That stops me, as you can see." He stood there with his penis limp.

"Oh, fudge!" Now she wept, her tears flowing copiously. "Please, I beg you. Can't you try?"

"No more than you can."

"I'll try!" she said. "I'll close my eyes and pretend you're a doctor."

"No."

"Or we can make it a game. The girls have rape fantasies. They want to be taken against their seeming will, but they really love it. Let me be the captive maiden and you the ardent hero. Come kiss me hard, and press against me, and I will melt."

Would that work? The pretense of a game? "All right."

He joined her on the bed, embraced her, and kissed her. She kissed him back, savagely. She pressed her lovely bare body against him.

His member swelled. It nudged her cleft.

She felt it and screamed.

So much for that. "I'll take you back to the village," he said.

"Yes," she agreed, sobbing. She put on her dress. "Why did you have to be a unicorn?"

"It's my curse," Wetzel said. "I could readily have made it with a non-virgin."

"You're a decent guy," she said as they went outside. "Too decent. If you had just forced me a little—"

"Impossible."

She paused. "Or could I force you? Suppose you just lie there, and I take the initiative."

"It wouldn't work."

"Come on. Let's try anyway."

Wetzel sighed inwardly. She would have to be shown.

They went back inside, and she stripped again. He lay on the bed on his back. She sat beside him and played with his member, making it respond. He was surprised she could do that. It seemed it wasn't the body that repelled her, but the act.

When she had him stiff, she mounted him. But the moment her cleft touched his member, she screamed again. His member sagged. She wasn't conscious of making a turn-off signal, but was doing it naturally. "I can't *do* it!" she wailed.

"You can't do it," he agreed. "Neither can I. It's the way it is, with a virgin and a unicorn. If we had a week it would be possible. I have done it with other virgins, when there was time. But never in hours, let alone minutes."

"Maybe your mission will take a week."

"Maybe it will."

"I'll keep trying."

"That's fine."

They went back outside, he transformed, she mounted, and he carried her back to the village. By then her bees had mopped up her tears and made her face presentable. They reentered the hall, where the dancing continued.

Wetzel saw Pinkie glance their way, nodding. He read it in her mind: The woman had known when they left, and that this would happen. She had let the girl learn the way she had to.

Another girl approached him. "I'm not a virgin," she murmured. "I too want a baby." Her red ants were not alarmed.

But Wetzel had had enough for this night. "Some other time."

"Squish it," she swore, turning away.

In due course the dance concluded, and they returned to their house to sleep.

"You fools passed up more hot chances," Vanja said. "If they were men, I'd have taken them all on."

"I would not," Veee said.

"Which is why I didn't," Tod said.

Wetzel felt the feather touch again. He touched his head with a finger, warning the others. They all put dangerous thoughts into their storm cellars.

The men had depended on a mechanical bug, and a door alarm. The women were using neither of these things—the team had quietly checked—but evidently had their own way to keep track. But they didn't know about Wetzel's telepathy. That was perhaps just as well. They were no more to be trusted than the men.

"Tomorrow we commune with the insects," Tod said. "Let's hope it gets us farther than before."

"Let's hope," Wizard agreed. "Pinkie said the insects are mildly telepathic. I presume that goes for the scarabs too. So they may indeed verify that we are here to help them."

"If we can," Tod said.

"The Amoeba sent us. That indicates that we can."

But could they really? Wetzel wasn't sure, and knew the others shared his doubt. This was a totally different mission from the last, requiring untested capacities. He had not been on the last one, but understood it had been a serious physical threat to animals and villagers alike, from a protoplasmic pool. Telepathy seemed to be the key this time, which meant it depended on Wetzel. He was not at all sure he was up to it.

Meanwhile his paradoxical private quest to find a marriageable permanent virgin remained stymied. He couldn't help himself; how could he help anyone else?

Discouraged, he slept.

CHAPTER 6: LADYBUG

In the morning they went to commune with the bugs. Pinkie showed them to a quiet glade in the forest, and they sat or lay on the soft moss, spread moderately apart. "You may talk, rest, or sleep, as you choose," Pinkie said. "The point is to let the bugs come to you. It may take a few minutes, or an hour, or a day. You need to stay in place until each of you has a bug." She was not speaking facetiously or dismissively; the term "bug" included more than insects and spiders. "You will know when it happens."

"Thank you," Tod said somewhat tersely.

Pinkie departed, leaving them to their communing. "I wonder what kind of bug I'll get?" Vanja said. "Maybe hornets. Then I could sic them on anyone who annoyed me."

"Or scorpions," Wizard said. "They can be beautiful and deadly."

"You're right," Vanja said. "My type."

"I'd prefer butterflies," Veee said. "They are artistic."

"I'd settle for the scarab," Tod said.

"Wouldn't we all," Wizard agreed. "Then we could address the next stage: how to save it from extinction."

"I have been thinking about that," Veee said. "I think what it needs is a refuge somewhere in the natural universe, where it can breed without being in danger from the poachers."

"Poachers can get anywhere anyone else can," Tod said.

"That's the problem," Wizard said. "We need either to mask the scarab's home planet so that the poachers can't find it, which I strongly suspect is beyond our powers to accomplish, or locate another world that will do. Then the problem would be finding that world, and verifying that it is suitable."

"We can find it through the Amoeba," Tod said. "And verify it if we have a scarab along."

"Which nicely validates our present quest," Wizard said. "One of us must befriend a scarab."

"Or be befriended by it," Veee said.

"And what if it doesn't choose to befriend any of us?" Vanja asked.

They lapsed into silence, unable to answer. Wetzel lay on his back and gazed at the sky, letting his mind go blank.

"Well, now," Tod said.

"You have a contact?" Veee asked.

"Yes. I have been befriended."

"Out with it!" Vanja said. "By what?"

"By ants."

"Ants!"

"Specifically, fire ants. I know them from my home frame. Small, reddish, and their bite burns for hours."

Vanja laughed. "They find you compatible? That must say something about your nature."

"Actually they are hard workers, and fair protection. Pinkie is right: they seem to have a bit of telepathy, so I know their sentiment. They do find me compatible. And, actually, I find them compatible, now that I know them."

"It's hilarious," Vanja said. Then: "Oh."

"You've found your bug?" Veee said.

"Mosquitoes."

They all laughed. Of course bloodsuckers would like the vampire. It did seem to serve her right.

Then Wizard spoke. "My turn. I have been adopted by a spider. I believe it is the brown recluse, one of the most poisonous known."

"That figures," Tod said. "You can use that poison in a potion."

"I'm not that kind of wizard. I do magic, not concoctions."

"But you see, now you *are* that kind," Vanja said. "You have what you lack. It may be useful."

"Just as your mosquitoes may be useful," Wizard retorted."

"Oh, my." It was Veee. "Flies."

"Well, as long as we're being brought low," Vanja said, "join the throng."

"Actually, they're rather pretty." Veee held one up on a finger. It was bright red and black. There were different colored ones on her hair.

"I know that kind," Tod said. "Flower flies. Maybe the prettiest of all flies. They don't sting; they visit flowers, like bees or butterflies."

"Yes," Veee agreed. "I like them."

"One to go," Vanja said. "How are you doing, Wetz? Find any grubs yet?"

Then Wetzel felt a feather mind touch. He had a sudden revelation. It wasn't human, it was insect! Could this be the scarab? "Give me a moment," he said. "This may be important."

The others were silent, giving him that moment.

"Who are you?" he sub-vocalized to focus his thought.

There was no direct answer, merely an awareness of his query. It did not seem to be avoidance so much as incapacity, as though the other mind was muzzled.

Maybe he could help. "Are you the scarab?" he asked.

That brought a faint answer. *May*be.

So far so good. "Have you come to join me?"

Now there was just uncertainty.

"Do you need to know me better?"

Yes.

"How can I help you to know me better?"

Help me.

That confused him. Maybe the bug could not answer directly. It might be complicated.

"I am Wetzel Were-Unicorn. I am telepathic."

Name me.

This remained odd, but seemed to be progress. "LadyBug." He flashed a picture of a pretty ladybug. That was not a scarab, but perhaps they were distantly related, being flying beetles.

There was an impression almost of humor. *Forelimb.*

Wetzel considered, then lifted his right hand to hover over his face as he lay.

A small insect flew to perch on his hand. A lovely ladybug. Exactly the kind he had pictured. Not a scarab.

"LadyBug," he said, addressing her. He knew she was a her; faint as it was, her mindset was female.

Wetzel. The thought was stronger now.

He buried his disappointment that she was not a scarab. She was his contact insect. That was what counted. "You are beautiful."

Look at me.

He looked more closely, bringing her near his face. Her outline fuzzed. She was not after all a ladybug. That was merely an emulation, honoring his mental picture. He focused more intently, trying to fathom her actual shape, but the fuzz remained. "You must help me," he said. "I can't see you clearly."

Open mind.

Oh. He had kept his mind guarded, but this was no enemy. He wanted her trust, so would have to extend his own. He released his guard, letting her in, as it were.

Then her outline clarified. She was a bug, globular, with rounded appendages and a snout. But not just any bug. She was—

His mind refocused, amazed.

This was THE bug. The fractal basis. The outline of the Mandelbrot set Tod had described.

Then he was plunging closer with his mind's eye, seeing not just the outline, but the phenomenally intricate extensions of it in two and a half dimensions. The closer he looked the more complicated it became. It was like descending to a planet and discovering ever more of its detail as the magnification multiplied. He realized that it was no longer really his eyes that were seeing it, but his mind, his telepathic rapport. LadyBug was showing him her true form.

Those were not hairs on the bug. They were rows of projections, each in the shape of a smaller bug, each twisting outward, forming ever-finer filaments. The bug was surrounded by jewel-like shapes composed of yet smaller and more intricate contours. They formed chains of twists, each delicately linked to the next. The connections between them were pinned by more bugs like the first one, only infinitely smaller. There seemed to be no end to it; the sequence was infinite. All of it was alive, pulsing with its own processes, shifting its finely meshing colors even as he focused. They made jewelry from the dead scarabs? They had only the crudest shell of its true éclat.

He was lost in the sheer wonder of it.

Wetzel.

She was calling him. He reluctantly shut his mental gaze and returned to the macroscopic realm. "LadyBug," he replied, gazing at his hand with the ladybug on it.

Now you know me as no other creature not of my own kind has. You have seen me nude.

"Thank you for that vision." He understood perfectly what she meant. "I was lost in your beauty."

You lent me your mind. Then I could show you.

"You showed me," he agreed. "LadyBug, you are the most fascinating creature I have ever seen."

You are the only one of your kind to see me thus.

"I am immensely privileged."

No one else must see.

Because any human being who saw her would want to possess her, squeezing the juice from her and making the empty shell into jewelry. That could not be tolerated. But there was a question. "What of my associates? They too want to rescue you."

They may know of me as LadyBug, but not see my true form.

"And how is it we are now communicating so much more effectively?"

You are lending me your huge mind and telepathy, amplifying my own. Alone I have little mind; with you I have enough. I owe it to you.

"Welcome to it, LadyBug."

Now I will perch on your head, where the contact will be strongest. I will show your associates only the ladybug form. She flew from his hand to his head as he sat up. He wasn't sure how she flew, because her real form seemed to have no wings. For that matter, he was similarly ignorant about how she walked, because she lacked legs. Did she even have eyes to see? Ears to hear?

I move my extensions. They are invisibly small to your gaze, but there are many, and they suffice. I can perceive the flexes in my surroundings that you refer to as light and sound. I can see and hear you well enough. My finer extensions reach into the realm of thought, enabling telepathy. Now tell your companions.

"I will introduce you," he agreed.

That is good. Now the thought was remarkably strong and clear. *Remember to warn them not to reveal my presence to others. It could cost me my life.*

It could indeed. "Folks," Wetzel said. "I want to introduce my contact, LadyBug. She is not as she appears, but must hide her true form for the sake of safety. She is a scarab, but we will refer to her only as LadyBug. We will not tell anyone else her identity, because no one else can be trusted to truly preserve her."

The others came to him, peering at his head. "Oh, she really is a ladybug!" Veee said. "From what I see."

"If I could see her as she is," Tod asked, "would I see the Mandlebrot set?"

"Yes, in all its infinite detail, extending from the physical basis to the nuances of thought. LadyBug is that shape, alive."

"I am awed."

I like him, as I see him reflected in your mind. I will make an exception.

"Look closely at her," Wetzel told Tod.

Tod looked. His face went slack. Wetzel knew from his mind that he was falling onto the planet, appreciating its marvelous detail. He was a fan of the Mandlebrot set, and this was a spirited version.

Enough.

Wetzel put his hand up, interrupting Tod's view of LadyBug. Tod's face resumed animation. "She really is," he breathed. "The most beautiful creature in the universe."

"She is," Wetzel agreed.

"It seems our roster is complete," Wizard said. "Now we can organize for the mission."

They returned to the village. "We have been befriended," Tod told Pinkie. "Each of us has a bug."

Each of them stepped before her, showing off their companions: ants, flower flies, mosquitoes, spider, and ladybug.

"Very nice," Pinkie said. "But no scarab."

"We are now able to contact the scarabs when we need to, via our friends," Tod said. "That should suffice."

"I suppose it should." She was plainly disappointed. "What is your next step?"

"We must ponder that," Tod said. "We are thinking of locating a secure retreat where the scarabs can mate and grow safely. This may not be easy to find."

"Not easy at all," Pinkie agreed.

They retreated to their house. "We shall need to clarify aspects with our associates," Wizard said. "Such as can we safely take showers when they are with us?" He looked at Wetzel.

"Let me formulate an opinion," Wetzel said. Then he communed with LadyBug. "Can we?"

Picture this ablution.

He did, imagining taking a hot shower, then combing out his hair.

This resembles a rainstorm. We bugs can handle that. Your hair and skin will shield us from the heat and motion of the water. We will avoid the comb and brush.

"Showers are okay," Wetzel announced.

"Next question," Vanja said. "What about sex? We can no longer go elsewhere to have it, since the bugs will be with us."

"Do you know about sex?" Wetzel asked LadyBug. "The villagers refrain from it so as not to drive you away."

We do. They do. We appreciate that. But you may do it.

"We may? How can that be?

The other bugs have no objection. Only we scarabs. But now I know you, and you may do it.

"I don't understand. If you can handle sex, why do you avoid the villagers when they practice it?"

Jealousy.

Wetzel thought he had misheard. "I still don't understand."

We are all females. We get the chance to breed only maybe once in a decade when there is a male, and only a few of us get to do it then. You humans do it so often and joyously that we can't stand it and have to retreat.

Oh. "But won't you be jealous if I do it with Vanja?"

Not if you let me share the experience.

"Again I have a confusion. How can you share it?"

Let me ride your mind and emotion. I will feel your feeling. I know already from your memories of prior occasions that I will revel in this vicarious experience. It will be much better than what I can anticipate on my own.

Wetzel nodded, physically and mentally. That did make sense.

"I believe I have the essence," Wetzel said to the others. "We can indulge in our normal lives, including sex; the bugs can handle it. They know us better; the proscription remains for the village as a whole. I should be able to answer questions by the others, as I am in close touch with LadyBug and she will answer through me. We should be able to plan our mission now."

"We need better background," Wizard said. "Why are the scarab so rare? Is it entirely the fault of the poachers?"

Wetzel relayed the question to LadyBug as he heard it, so that it was as if Wizard were speaking directly to her. Then Wetzel answered for her. "Yes. The scarabs are inedible and harmless to others, so are not preyed upon by animals for food or self-defense. They were plentiful until their beauty and chemical properties were discovered by human beings. In twenty years predation was so bad they were reduced to perhaps a hundredth of their former number, and that continues. Only one in ten survive to adulthood in ten years. The Amoeba interceded by making itself a refuge, and that helped. But because there are no males here—males can't survive within the Amoeba, for reasons we don't understand—breeding must take place on the home planet, and that is where the poachers are. Without males the scarab will become extinct within a decade."

"I gather the males are rarer than the females," Wizard said. "Why is this so?"

"This relates to their life cycle," Wetzel said, relaying it as he learned it. "One male can mate with one female every year or so; it takes him a while to recharge. He can do that for about thirty years before he dies. Each female that is bred fissions into about a hundred infant scarabs, who will in the course of a decade and four molts become adult and able to breed. She is then breedable for about thirty years, if she encounters a male. But there are no males here in the Amoeba; they must leave the Amoeba to have any hope of breeding."

"This talk of breeding is getting to me," Vanja said. "Let's take a break."

"We will resume this discussion in the morning," Tod said.

They took their showers, and none of the bugs were bothered. They made temporary shelters from the hair of their hosts.

Then Pinkie came to invite them to the evening meal, and they went. The women openly admired the bugs; now the team was similar to the villagers in that respect. Even Vanja's mosquitoes were well behaved, threatening no one. Younger women continued to flirt with the men, interested in trysts away from the village. The men continued to decline with evident regret.

Back at the house, in the evening, Tod remembered something. "We may be able to have sex, but the village stricture remains, and we should not violate it. They might misunderstand."

Veee nodded. "The good ladies might want to know how we know that it's all right."

"For us and not for them," Tod said, faintly smiling.

"And we shall have no viable answer," Wizard said.

Vanja was ready. "Give me a unicorn ride, Wetz."

Veee sighed. "We shall hold the home fortress."

The two of them went out, and transformed, and raced to the official Village Love Nest. It was unoccupied, unsurprisingly. They transformed back to human form, and entered, neither having any need to strip off clothing.

Vanja stepped into him and kissed him. "It's lust, not love, but I am getting to like you, Wetzel."

"It's my unicorn quality. It attracts all women except virgins."

Virgins? LadyBug inquired.

Uh-oh. "I need to discuss virginity," Wetzel told Vanja.

"I'm no good for that," Vanja said, smiling. "I'm not sure I ever was one."

"A virgin is a woman who has never indulged in sex," Wetzel explained to LadyBug. "Once she has sex, she is no longer a virgin. I am desperately attracted to virgins, but they are not attracted to me. This can be awkward."

I am a virgin.

"Yes, you are virginal. Do you prefer that Vanja and I not do this?"

Not at all. My kind has no non-virgins. We all crave fulfillment, though it destroys us.

"So you do not follow the rule of the unicorn. You are net repelled by my interest in sex."

Neither repelled nor attracted. I am an insect. We are governed by different rules.

"Yet you have a problem when other human couples indulge in sex."

True. Now that I am sharing your mind, being vastly enhanced by it, I suspect I am sharing also your propensities. I never shared a human mind before.

"In that case, Vanja and I will proceed. But let me know if this becomes objectionable to you."

Get on with it.

Wetzel smiled. "We're fit to proceed," he told Vanja.

"So I heard, from your half of the dialogue. I wonder—could I talk with Ladybug, if we had reason to talk?"

"I don't think so. She could read your mind if she sat on your head, but her ability to project is limited to things like Go Away. That's how the surviving scarabs have managed to avoid capture."

"I understand that. But if you enhanced her ability to project, so she could project to me?"

"I had not thought of that. I don't know."

I might.

"She might. We can try it, if you wish."

"Try it."

"LadyBug, see if you can draw on my telepathic power to project your thoughts to Vanja. Such an ability might be important."

Hello, Vanja.

Vanja was startled. "I got that!"

"You can focus your thought to her by speaking it, Vanja, as I do. Or you can simply think hard, and she will read it via my telepathy."

Hello LadyBug. Vanja thought. Wetzel got it because it was his telepathy being used to read it.

You are a bat!

"Yes. You saw me transform. But I don't eat my friends." Vanja found it easier to vocalize.

What is a friend?

"That is when two people—by people I mean anyone of any kind, human, unicorn, bat or bug—come to know each other, and to like each other. Wetzel and I are friends. We understand each other. We are both were-creatures."

Can I be a friend? This concept is unknown in my species.

"When you borrow Wetzel's mind, you can understand friendship," Vanja said. "Then it becomes possible for you."

I want to be a friend.

"We'll be your friends," Wetzel said. "That means in part that if you should get in trouble, we would try to help you."

"If you broke a wing and could not fly," Vanja said, "I could transform to bat form and carry you to safety. I would not eat you because you are my friend, and you would trust me for the same reason."

I don't know how I could help you if you were in trouble, but I would try.

"You can help us by enabling us to save your species," Wetzel said. "That is our mission."

Now will you have sex?

Wetzel and Vanja laughed.

"We had better do it slowly, and explain the steps, so she can understand it throughout," Vanja said.

Wetzel approached her where she stood. He saw the mosquitoes perched on her hair, and hesitated.

"They won't bite you," Vanja said. "They don't suck the blood of friends."

He laughed. "Of course not. But do they get jealous?"

"They don't care about what else I do. They don't have the intellect or power of the scarabs. They are lesser creatures, content with their lot."

"Then I will kiss you. This is a precursor to sex." He held her close and kissed her.

I feel a surge of emotion.

"The kiss does arouse interest and expectation," Wetzel said. "If she were not interested, she would avoid the kiss, or break away following it. It is a kind of courtship."

Courtship?

"The man woos the woman," Vanja explained. "He flatters her, so that she will give him sex. She knows that's all he really wants, but she likes his attention anyway."

Even if she is a virgin?

"Even then, normally. Why virgins don't want sex with were-unicorns is a mystery."

Because they know they will lose their virginity and his interest. So they make him work for it, giving them more attention than they would have otherwise.

"Mystery solved!" Vanja said appreciatively.

An insect had quickly solved a riddle Wetzel had not fathomed with all his thought? Maybe it came with the territory of being virginal or dead.

May I borrow your body?

Vanja smiled. "That depends on what you want to do with it."

Not to do; to feel. I want to feel your feeling while you do the sex.

"Welcome."

Thank you. I will reach for you with Wetzel's telepathy, which is far stronger than mine.

Then something subtly changed. Vanja remained the same, physically, but her mood shifted. "Well, now," she murmured. "That is strange and wonderful."

Wetzel, still holding her, suddenly realized what it was. "You're a virgin!" he exclaimed.

I am, LadyBug thought. *Her body is not, but I am.*

"It is the emotion that counts," Wetzel said, his interest intensifying. "I pick it up telepathically." He was embracing a virgin in spirit!

"Take it, LadyBug," Vanja said, intrigued.

I do not know what to do. I thought only to watch and learn.

Vanja, reveling in the feeling, neither acted nor spoke. She was being a passive virgin, a prohibitively rare experience for her. She was largely lost in the wonder of it.

"I do know," Wetzel said. "You can experience the sex for yourself." He slid his hands down to Vanja's sculptured bottom, squeezing the buttocks. "The feel of her flesh excites me," he said, though LadyBug was surely reading that directly. "It makes my copulatory member swell."

She was reading it. *That excites this body too.*

Then he drew back and put his mouth to her breasts, kissing the nipples. "This turns me on further."

I do not know what that flesh is, or what it does, but your caress generates a hunger I have never before felt.

Then, unable to delay longer, he guided Vanja to the bed, laid her on her back, mounted her, and carefully entered her. "I am causing that member to penetrate her body. I am inserting it to its full length." He kissed her as he drove into her core and spurted. "I am ejaculating!" he gasped. "The reproductive fluid is passing from me to her."

Glorious!

"Glorious," Vanja echoed, experiencing his orgasm via the telepathic connection. "So urgent! So robust! I never felt what a male feels."

What does a female feel?

"We'll show you," Wetzel said. He withdrew, then moved down to put his face on Vanja's cleft. He tongued it.

She was already well worked up. In moments she went into her own orgasm, her thighs clamping on his head. It was less intense than his, but lasted longer, and was fully as satisfying.

I am ready to die.

Both Wetzel and Vanja reacted with alarm. "Mating makes you fission!" Wetzel said.

I did not breed. I experienced your mating. I have no maleseed. I can't fission.

They relaxed. "And we must find a scarab male for you to breed with," Wetzel said. "And a safe haven for that breeding to occur. That is our mission."

They lay for a while, the three of them savoring the experience. Then Wetzel thought of something. "You're not a virgin any more, LadyBug," he said regretfully.

But I am. My body has not been bred.

"But you just experienced two orgasms."

They were yours, not mine. When I get mine, I will happily fission and die. At least now I know what it will be like.

Wetzel checked her mind. She was now that anomaly, an

experienced virgin. "Amazing."

"Wetzel, you have your permanent virgin!" Vanja said.

That made him pause. Could it be? But he realized that it wasn't. "It is a mock-up, fashioned from a vampire and a beetle. Not someone I can marry and sire children with."

"I could bear you babies."

"But after LadyBug passes from the scene, either by breeding or old age, then the virginity would be gone, and I would have little interest in remaining with you, or you with me. We're not for each other Vanja, in that manner."

She sighed. "We're not."

We're not, LadyBug agreed with similar regret.

"Meanwhile we still have serious problems to work out," Wetzel said. "Such as how to find a male scarab, and how to locate a poacher-free world that is suitable for scarab reproduction."

"Which do we do first?" Vanja asked. "Neither one is much good without the other."

"Maybe the others can figure that out," Wetzel said. "We'd better go rejoin them."

He and Vanja transformed, and he galloped back along the path. It had been an interesting diversion, but now they did have work to do.

"What business do you have with the villagers?" Wetzel asked LadyBug, mentally vocalizing, as he could not speak in this form. It seemed to work well enough; it was the thought that counted, not the sound. "They avoid sex in the village so you won't be repelled, but why should you go there anyway?"

When we die of old age or injury we go there. Ordinarily we would linger and be uncomfortable. They kill us quickly and painlessly. In return they get to squeeze us and use our shells.

"They get your juice?" he asked, surprised.

Yes. It is valuable to them.

"It is. They get a lot of money for it."

Money?

"Wealth. They can buy many things they want."

Buy?

Wetzel tried again. "The way you want to breed and fulfill your destiny, they want to get money. That is their fulfillment."

Strange.

"We are not like scarabs," he reminded her. "The poachers want money too. That's why they chase you."

We thought they just hated us.

"No, it's for money. Money drives human cultures."

Maybe in time, with your mind, I will comprehend that.

Wetzel changed the subject. "Why are there so few scarab males?"

It is our way. One male breeds many females, so we need few males. We do not know who they are until the fourth molt. Maybe it is not decided until then. By that time only one in ten of us survives, and often there is no male left in that brood. There was none in mine. Of course I would not breed with a male of my own brood, but with a male of another brood. But they all bred elsewhere and none was left for me.

"So it may be hard for us to find a male."

Very hard, she agreed.

"Those molts," he asked. "What is their nature?"

They define the four stages of our existence. When we first appear, the result of the fissioning of our parent, we are very small. We float in air, drifting with the winds, eating what we encounter, slowly increasing our mass. It is our amoeba stage. When we become too large to float, we land on the ground and molt, assuming our second form. We are in our slug stage, crawling on slime to reach the flowers. We must find pollen to feed on so we can survive and grow. When we are large enough, after two or three years, we molt and form into our third form, caterpillars, with many legs, and can travel much faster and feed better. We grow again, and in another two to three years we molt and assume our adult form, with wings and shell. By ten years most of us are full scarabs. This is when we become male and female. We can breed at that point, immediately or any time before we die of old age. I am thirty; I have ten more years to breed if I am going to.

This is remarkable, Vanja thought. Wetzel had included her in the dialogue, but in bat form she could not speak in human language. *LadyBug is a middle aged female.* Then, to LadyBug: *What are your males like? How do they breed you?*

Wetzel kept mentally silent. Naturally the vampire was interested in sex, however it occurred. But he was curious too.

The male scarab is like the female, but larger. That makes him more obvious, and the poachers catch males more readily. To breed a female he pokes his snout into her nether crevice and pumps her so full of semen that she explodes.

"That must be a lot of semen!"

It almost matches her mass. That's why it takes him a year to build up another load. She inflates, her every portion swelling, and holds together until the internal pressure is too great, then lets go and gloriously fissions.

"To receive that much ejaculate!" Vanja subvocalized, now emulating Wetzel's technique in bat form. "That must be some thrill. I envy you that experience, LadyBug; no male I know puts out volume like that. But couldn't you stop partway through, so as not to detonate?"

Why would I want to? It is the fulfillment of my destiny.

"So it seems." Vanja paused, considering. "Wetzel, if I assumed human form, and you assumed unicorn form, how much ejaculate could you squeeze into me?"

What a notion! "Not enough to make you burst. It would leak out, because your channel doesn't lead to your interior body in that manner."

"Well, if you put it to the hole that does lead there—"

"No."

"You're a damned prude."

Wetzel realized he was. So he changed the subject. "LadyBug, is the special nature of your—your juice—something that develops in your maturity? So that you aren't so much at risk as you grow?"

No. It is viable throughout our life cycle, and our young forms are easier to squish. But at first we are too small for the poachers to catch, so we survive. But by the third molt we are easy prey. They pick us up from the ground and trees, and we can't avoid them. Only as adults, when we can fly and broadcast Leave-Me-Alone thoughts, are we able to avoid them, and then imperfectly. They have developed immunity to our repulsion thoughts. They set traps to snare us, and they set fires to drive us into their nets. We are helpless before them.

"We have to find you a safe refuge," Wetzel subvocalized.

"Amen," Vanja agreed.

They reached the town, transformed, and reentered the house.

"How was it?" Veee asked.

"Amazing," Vanja said. "LadyBug shared the experience."

"She what?" Tod asked.

"She linked with us mentally, and felt our orgasms. She loved it."

"But she can't have sex!" Tod exclaimed.

"Mentally she can," Wetzel said. "It's the actual breeding with a male scarab that causes her to fission. That's a—a physical thing, rather than a mental or emotional one."

"Oh, vicarious," Veee said.

"Not exactly, but close enough. So she enjoyed our activity without suffering damage."

"Meanwhile, while traveling, we learned more," Vanja said. "We've got to find a suitable refuge for the scarabs, and put some males in it."

"That, I think, is our first priority," Tod said. "The refuge. Finding males will do no good unless we have a safe haven for them, where they can breed."

"And we have no idea where it may be," Veee said.

There was a knock on the door. Another comely young woman was there, featuring deep red hair, with matching red pupils. It was the red-ant girl who had approached him the night before, shapely and sure of herself. "I am Paige. I would like to ride the unicorn," she said.

Wetzel read her mind. It was a figure of speech. She did want a ride, but she also wanted sex. She was not a virgin, as she had told him before. But he was tired, and though she was lovely, she did not appeal to him the way a virgin did. "I regret, no."

"But I can pay for it," Paige said. "I have information I think you need."

"What would that be?" Wetzel asked.

"The location of the access to a world where scarabs might live."

Suddenly she had the attention of all of them. Wetzel glanced at Tod. Tod nodded, his mind emphatic.

"Give her the ride," Veee said.

They knew that such close contact would enable him to read the girl's mind and get her information. Giving her what she wanted would be a fair exchange.

"It's a deal," Wetzel said, his tiredness dissipated

CHAPTER 7: REFUGE

—————

They went outside, Wetzel transformed to unicorn, and Paige lithely leaped on. He read it in her mind: she had ridden horses. He also read her slight disappointment that she had not been able to seduce Tod; for one thing he now had ants, as she did. But the prospect of trying for a baby excited her more.

As he trotted toward the Love Nest he read more: she did know of an access to a special world where scarabs might prosper. The women knew about it, but for some reason dismissed it as a prospect. Why? Wetzel could not fathom the reason, because it was not in her conscious mind at the moment. She was merely using the information as a way to get sex from him, having had the wit to think of this when the other women hadn't. He had to respect her smartness in this respect.

They arrived at the Nest. Paige dismounted, he transformed to manform, and they entered the house. She immediately stripped naked, completely ready for action.

"First things first," Wetzel said, though her appearance and eagerness did turn him on, as his rising penis showed. Non-virgins did have their points, especially when they were as young and pretty as this. "Where is this access, and how do you know scarabs might prosper there?"

"How about this deal: do me this instant. Then I will tell you all about it. Then you can do me again before we go, to increase the likelihood it will take."

She wanted to be sure she did get bred. She could not read his mind, so feared there would be some slip-up, as she knew there had been with virginal Pisa.

"Fair enough."

"I'll choose the position for the first time. You choose for the second."

"Fair enough," he repeated.

She got on the bed on her hands and knees, then put her head down so that only her plump rump was high. "This way." It was in her mind that the ejaculate would pool below, instead of leaking out.

He mounted her from behind, found the place, and shoved down in, knowing that she did not want love-play, only semen. Her anticipation had already made her wet. By the third thrust he was spurting vigorously into her. This was actually a business transaction, but he did enjoy it as he enjoyed any interaction with a comely woman. It lacked the edge of sex with a virgin, but that did not make it unpalatable. Not at all!

"Ooooh," she moaned, grateful not for the sex so much as the copious life-promising fluid. She had neither had nor desired an orgasm. But she wanted him to think his sexual prowess had turned her on, knowing that men liked to believe in that sort of thing. This was of course part of the non-virgin syndrome, teasing men into better performance.

He picked up a secondary mental state. It was the red ants. Paige was not telepathic, but they were, and appreciated not her artistry so much as his powerful broadcast of bliss as he climaxed, just as LadyBug did.

They are females too, LadyBug thought. *They don't get to breed, but wish they could.*

Yet another nuance to appreciate.

They held the position, letting the last of the fluid transfer. Then he withdrew, carefully. She remained as she was for a time, making sure.

Finally Paige got up and dressed without washing, knowing that there would be more sex soon. She consciously clenched her vagina to hold in the thickening substance. Wetzel, reading her mind, was intrigued; this was a side of a woman he had not seen before. Vanja had no compunction about cleaning herself out after sex, and neither had Weava before her. He hadn't stayed with the other village women long enough to pick up on what they did post-coitus. For them the sex itself was important, not the aftermath, and certainly not any thought of conceiving.

Paige flashed a smile at him. "This way."

She led him out the back door. There was what appeared to be a wishing well, a small stone structure with a cover and a roped bucket. "Look," she said, indicating the well.

He peered down into it. Instead of water below there appeared to be a plug of fog. "What is it?"

"A kind of cloud, as far as we know. A portal to another world. We have lowered animals into it and brought them back up and they have been fine. We have loosed birds there and they have not returned except for one bound by a string on a foot. When we hauled it back it was fine. In fact when we untied the string it plunged into the well, returning to that world by choice. Once we tied the feet of a daring woman and lowered her headfirst through it, and she reported that the air is breathable and she thinks the gravity is normal, and the temperature, but she couldn't see past the mist. She wanted to use a longer rope, but we feared danger. We have not dared go farther. But it seems like a world where bugs could prosper."

"Why didn't you send scarabs through?"

"What would be the point, without males? They would live for a while and die. So we wrote it off as a prospect. It's a false lead, unusable. But your team, with your bat—maybe she could fly there and verify it. Then you would know."

"It's a great prospect, Paige," he said enthusiastically. He embraced her and kissed her on the mouth. "We'll do that. Thank you."

"I'm glad I thought of it," she said, pleased. "If, after this is over, you wish to settle down, I would be happy to marry you." Her mind revealed that this was a calculated ploy: she would get chronic breeding, support for her children, and perhaps even love. She would be the envy of all the villagers. She would in return make sure he was sexually satisfied. In fact she might even lend him to friends, as favors, during her pregnancies. She could thus work her way up to village chief, in due course.

Wetzel was sure that there would be many men who would gladly settle for that deal. But he could not: she wasn't a virgin. "I appreciate the offer, but I am committed to the team."

"You and Tod," she said, grimacing prettily.

They went back inside the house. She stripped again and lay on the bed face-up, anticipating his preference. He kissed her breasts, then mounted her and entered, again with no other foreplay, as she would have tolerated that only to keep her word. She just wanted it done so she could go home and hope for her baby. And, in a moment it was done. She now had a double load of semen.

Soon they were on their way back. It had been a worthwhile interlude, entirely apart from the sex. Each of them had gotten what they wanted.

At the village Paige dismounted, he transformed, and they separated. Veee had shorts waiting for him inside.

"There is a portal," he said. "It's behind the Love Nest, masked as a wishing well. Breathable air, comfortable temperature, but they have not been able to see it. Vanja should be able to explore it and let us know."

"Tomorrow," Tod said.

Vanja joined him in bed. "She worked you over," she said. "You know I regard that as a challenge."

He knew. He let her address him, and soon he was climaxing a third time that evening. It was interesting comparing techniques of non-virgins.

"Now tell me the truth: how did it compare?"

"You are a much better sexual partner than she is. I read in her mind that though she would accommodate me if I wished, all she wanted was my seed in her. So I delivered it without foreplay; I simply shoved in and spurted. Twice. You, in contrast, do it for fun, and that is fun for me too."

"You're not just mindreading what I want to hear?"

"Tell her, LadyBug," he said.

He would rather be with you than any woman except a virgin. He likes you.

"That will do," Vanja said, and spread herself against him for sleep. And, as she intended, that body contact and her mental eagerness slowly worked him up again, and they had sex during an intermission from sleep. Which was of course another thing he liked about her. She wanted to match the two times he had done it with Paige, but to do so from his desire rather than hers. So she quietly evoked his renewed desire. All that was in her mind, and it enhanced his interest.

In the morning they organized for the exploration. Tod was open about it, bracing Pinkie. "We have learned of the portal to another planet. We wish to explore it to see whether it is suitable for scarabs, and whether it is secure from poachers. Do we have your approval?"

"That world will do you no good," she said. "You need to get at least one male scarab, and that male can't cross the Amoeba. So even if it is ideal, it's useless. That's why I didn't think to mention it."

"We want to check it anyway. If it seems good, then we will tackle the problem of conveying a male scarab there." Tod smiled. "Then we will see about finding one. It may seem haphazard, but we are amateurs finding our way."

"That I can see." But she smiled back. Her mind indicated that she was within breeding age and would do it if she ever got the chance, with whatever man was available. She knew about Paige's tryst, and was casting about to get similar trysts for herself and the other women of the village. If cooperating with the portal exploration meant the men would remain here longer, she approved.

"Thank you," Tod said. "Wetzel, would you care to give this lady a ride to the portal, so she can supervise our effort?"

Stroke of genius! Wetzel gave his shorts to Veee and transformed. Tod helped Pinkie mount. She was not an experienced rider, but he could handle that. He walked sedately, carrying her, and though she maintained a sober facial expression, she was completely thrilled.

The others walked, joined by a number of the village women.

They all knew of Paige's accomplishment, and all hoped for something similar. Maybe if one of them managed to help in a way the men appreciated . . .

At the Love Nest Pinkie took over. She had the women bring out a pulley framework and a thick coil of rope attached to a hanging seat. "We do not know the end of the fog," she said. "But we presume there *is* an end. This is all the rope we have, and it does not reach below the fog. But if your bat can fly out of the fog, and return, then you will know." She frowned. "I do not recommend this course. There could be danger."

"We'll risk it," Vanja said. Her mind was revving up; she liked the thrill of the unknown, and of danger.

Vanja sat in the chair, and Tod cranked her slowly down into the well. "Do not go far," he said. "We can't follow you to help if you get lost."

"I won't get lost," she said confidently. Then, to Wetzel: *Track me. If I do get lost, you can be a beacon.*

Wetzel nodded. He would stay in mental touch with her, using LadyBug's ability to send out thoughts.

Vanja disappeared into the well, and then into the fog at its base. *Nothing but darkness here.*

Wetzel sent a reassuring mood.

When the rope reached its limit, and the descent stopped, Vanja transformed. *I'm taking off. I'm using echolocation to be sure I don't crash into anything, but there's nothing.*

"She will now explore in bat form," Tod said as the rope went slack.

I'm out of the fog! Bright sky! It was a cloud I was in, sitting at the top of a mountain. Green trees, mountains, rivers, fields—it's a verdant world! And there are insects here; I just ate one. Scarabs could live here.

Then something odd occurred. Vanja's thoughts seemed to accelerate until they became unintelligible. Was there some kind of interference? Best to get her out of there quickly.

Come back now, Wetzel thought. *We have enough to assimilate.*

Awww, she complained. But she turned about and flew back to the cloud, and to the hanging chair, which her echolocation spotted. She transformed, and Tod, feeling the rope go taut with her resumed weight, began cranking her back up.

"It was great," she said as she emerged. "I explored for a good fifteen minutes. There's a perfect world there."

Fifteen minutes? She had been gone only a few seconds. But Wetzel elected not to make an issue of that until he had some better understanding. Something had happened, but Vanja seemed normal now.

They discussed it. "And the cloud sits atop a mountain?" Tod asked. "How much of a drop to the ground?"

"To the trees. It's almost brushing their top foliage, which is impenetrably thick. Just a little more rope and we could step from the chair to a branch, then climb down the tree."

"Then let's do it," Tod said. "We need to explore this world in more detail."

"One question," Veee said. "How do we get back to the cloud after we drop out of it?"

"I can fly up and tell them we're coming," Vanja said. "They can lower the chair on a longer rope."

"It seems feasible," Tod said.

"I think this is not for me," Wizard said. "I'm not good at rough country exploration. Better I remain here, and Vanja can notify me if my powers should be needed."

"We shall be happy to entertain you while you wait," Pinkie said warmly. She had seduction in mind, involving one or more of the nubile girls. Wizard knew it, and was not strongly disinclined. There were worse things than passing time with a number of interested women.

They were doing it immediately? Wetzel wasn't entirely easy with this, but had no objection he could make without generating needless alarm.

Vanja went down again, then Tod, then Veee, then Wetzel. They were out of immediate mind range, but he knew that would be restored once he joined them below.

He waited until the chair's descent stopped, then got off it, held onto it with his hands, and hung below it. Then he dropped. The distance was farther than he anticipated, but Vanja was right: the foliage of the tree was thick, and buoyed him until he could grasp a branch. He was in bright light.

Veee was there waiting for him. "Tod fell a little farther, and is wending his way on down," she said. "Vanja is watching out for him in bat form."

"Good enough," he said. "We'll follow."

"The cloud is moving."

It took him a moment to assimilate her meaning. Then he looked up at the gray cloud he had just dropped from. It was not at the top of the mountain, but to the side. That was why he had dropped farther than expected.

Then he got the rest of it from her mind. *The portal was in the cloud.* "The portal is moving out of reach," he said.

"We may have a problem getting back."

"Vanja can fly up there and warn them." Then he reconsidered. "That still won't help us. They don't have nearly enough rope to reach to the ground beyond the mountain."

"Let's wait and see how it looks later," she said.

They climbed down the tree, finding their way to its sturdy central trunk. Veee was surprisingly good at this; she had muscles where it counted. She must have climbed many trees in her original life.

Finally they reached the ground. There were Tod and Vanja. Tod opened his mouth to speak.

There was a horrendous roar. A giant lizard charged out of the brush, teeth snapping. It was going for Veee.

Wetzel didn't even think before he acted. He transformed to unicorn and stepped between Veee and the lizard. He lowered his deadly horn.

The lizard evidently had not encountered a unicorn before. It continued its charge.

Wetzel judged he massed only about half what the lizard did, but his weapon was highly effective against flesh. He braced himself for the impact. The lizard would run right onto the horn and be lethally impaled by its own momentum.

But the shock didn't come. At the last moment the lizard veered aside and ran on past without attacking. Wetzel turned to watch it, bemused, as it charged on across the plain that opened out in that direction. Why had it changed its dim mind?

I repelled it.

Oh. That did seem to be better. "Thanks, LadyBug," he mentally vocalized. "That is better than mayhem." He reverted to manform.

"The dinosaur avoided you," Veee said, surprised. He got from her mind that a dinosaur was a big reptile of Earth's distant past. She had learned this from Tod, who knew about such things. It seemed their scientists had found the bones.

"LadyBug repelled it. She can send negative thoughts, enhanced by my mind."

"Yes, that is how they avoid capture," Veee agreed. "I did not realize it would work against such a massive creature."

"It works," Wetzel said. "We can demonstrate." With LadyBug's help he sent her a Go Away thought.

Veee walked away from them.

Wetzel reversed it, and Veee turned around and approached. "Yes, I felt the mind touches, but responded anyway."

"You can block them, he reminded her. "If anything else tries to make you do something you do not wish to, like the mind monster . . ."

"Yes. I will be on guard."

"Now we'd better rejoin the others." Tod and Vanja had scattered in another direction when the lizard charged. Wetzel saw them returning.

There was a rumble. The ground shook. A widening crevice opened between the two couples.

"Earthquake!" Tod called. "Get away from it!" He and Vanja retreated again.

"Mount me!" Wetzel told Veee, and transformed back to unicorn. He stepped close to her; she dived onto his back, then scrambled to right herself. She had never ridden a horse, but was lithe and strong and caught on rapidly. She caught hold of his mane.

He trotted away from the crevice. He felt the ground quivering under his hooves and realized that the quake was growing faster than his trot. He broke into a gallop while Veee hung on. The ground continued to be shaky, but that diminished as he outdistanced the effect. He found firmer footing, but continued moving at speed, uncertain how far away was safe.

Indeed, he saw a lattice of cracks appearing on the plain to either side. They were not safe at all. He had to veer to thread between the churning crevices, and the ground was losing cohesion.

"The trees!" Veee said. "They are not shaking!"

Now he saw that the trees were virtual islands of stability. The ground cracked all around them, but not under them. Their roots might be holding the ground together. This was evidently a regular thing, because grass was growing there, while farther out it was just sand.

He ran for the nearest large tree. It had hugely spreading branches, marking its territory. He felt the ground firm up in its vicinity. This was an island of stability.

Veee slid off, landing neatly on the turf. Wetzel changed back to manform. "Now we're safe," he said, relieved.

"Not yet."

He followed her gaze. There was the lizard, heading for their same tree. "We can repel it"

"It needs to live too. We should let it come here."

She had sympathy for all living things. "Then we'd better climb the tree."

He boosted her up to the lowest branch. Then she wrapped her limbs around it and extended an arm down for him. He grasped it and hauled himself up to the branch. The two of them straddled it, then ascended to a higher branch.

Just in time, for the beast had arrived. It circled the trunk and lay down, its snout almost touching the tip of its tail. It seemed unaware of them.

No: its mind was perfectly aware of them, but it knew it could not reach them on the branch they were on. So, catlike, it ignored them, until such time as they dropped to the ground. Its first priority at the moment was safety.

"I think we have to wait a while," Wetzel said. "Do you really prefer to save the life of a creature who would gobble you down the moment you got in reach?"

"Yes, if it is not threatening me. It lives according to its nature, as we do."

I like this person.

"So do I," Wetzel agreed.

"I heard that," Veee said, surprised.

"LadyBug shared her thought with you. She can do that, in my ambiance."

"Should she have to leave you, she will be welcome to join me. My flower flies would not mind."

I will do that, if I have to.

"Meanwhile we have an assessment of this world," Wetzel said. "It is unsuitable for colonization, because it is too dangerous. Because of the lizards and quakes."

No. This world is fine for scarabs. The dinosaurs and quakes don't prey on bugs.

"Which is the point," Veee said. "We don't want humans here, because they do prey on scarabs."

"I stand corrected," Wetzel said. "This world is ideal."

A bat flew toward them. It was Vanja. *You folk all right?*

"We're fine," Veee answered. "We decided to rest in the tree. How is Tod?"

We found our own tree. Naturally I worked him over.

"Naturally," Veee agreed. There was no trace of jealousy in her mind. She and the vampire had come to terms long ago, and shared Tod as convenient.

Wetzel was satisfied to have Veee instead as a friend, not a lover. It was unusual, for him, but worthwhile.

It is, LadyBug agreed.

Vanja perched on the branch, transformed, and straddled it. "Tod thinks this planet is too tectonic for human colonization."

"We agree," Wetzel said. "But it's ideal for scarabs."

"Good enough," Vanja said. "Now all we need to do is find our way back to the Amoeba."

"Tod will be figuring that out," Veee said.

"He is. He says the portal cloud drifts at a set rate, on a set route, allowing the planet to rotate under it, and will return to the mountain we found it on in about four days. All we need to do is be there. And find a way to jump high enough."

"We'll work on that challenge," Wetzel said dryly.

"Do that." Vanja transformed and flew away.

"Actually she could fly up to the portal ahead of time, and tell Wizard," Veee said. "Wizard could then do telekinesis magic and lift us up."

"That seems good," Wetzel agreed. He had yet to see any of Wizard's magic personally, other than brief illusion, but the others believed in it.

"We do," Veee said.

Meanwhile the shaking had stopped. The quake had passed.

"Now you can tell the dinosaur to go," Veee said.

Oh. They could not descend from the tree until the big lizard was gone.

Go Away LadyBug thought.

The reptile roused itself, uncoiled from around the tree, and set out across the now-stable plain. It did not even know it had been directed.

They dropped down. Wetzel converted, and carried Veee across the plain, the way they had come. The ground was firm throughout.

LadyBug located Vanja's mind, and they homed in on her. *I love possessing such long-range telepathy. I could never do it without you.*

"I like being able to send thoughts," Wetzel said. "I can't do that without you."

We make a good team.

"We do."

I wish I could be your woman.

Veee laughed, not unsympathetically. "Sometimes friendship is worth more than sex."

Yes. I wish for friendship and *sex, as he has with Vanja. But I can do it only vicariously. There can never by physical sex between us. In fact, away from him, I can't even sustain the concepts. I'm a bug.*

Veee was sympathetic. "You're a person in bug form. Picture yourself as a svelte human female. Then he can picture himself with you: a virgin."

Wetzel stayed out of it.

They reached the other pair. "About time you got here," Vanja said. "This man is wearing me out."

"We haven't done it since you returned," Tod protested.

"Exactly."

They all laughed. Then they foraged for berries and fruits, finding plenty. They would not go hungry here.

They planned their strategy: remain in this area, on the slope of the mountain, until the cloud returned. Then Vanja would fly into it, notify Wizard, and he would levitate them to the hanging chair one by one.

Night was falling. They concluded that their best bet was to sleep in a big tree. That would be safe from large reptiles, and from quakes. They quested for the right tree, near the top of the mountain, big enough and with spreading branches to hold them all comfortably.

Evening was a surprise. When the light from the sun dropped beyond the horizon, they saw the night sky in all its splendor. There was no moon, but an almost solid array of burningly bright stars, so that they could see almost as well as in daylight.

"This must be in a star cluster," Tod said. "Tightly packed stars. It should be hard to access from normal space, which lessens the likelihood of pirates. But will that bother the scarabs?"

No. We forage by night as well as day.

They found two suitable nest sites, which they padded out with ferns. Wetzel expected Vanja to join him, but it was Veee. "I made a deal with LadyBug," she explained. But she had hidden that deal in her storm cellar.

Wetzel didn't argue; she was entitled to her privacy. They settled down embraced not for sex but for warmth and security in the center of the nest. He closed his eyes.

There before him stood a lovely young woman who vaguely resembled Veee but was not. *Hello, Wetzel.*

"LadyBug!"

Veee is lending me the semblance of her body so I can be with you.

He did not question it. "Then we can interact as humans."

Yes. Kiss me.

He took her in his arms and kissed her. In reality Veee was in his arms, but he was not kissing her. This was imagination buttressed by telepathy. The kiss did feel real, and was pleasant.

I am a virgin, she reminded him.

Indeed she was. His interest intensified. He kissed her again, and she kissed him back and pressed her virginal breasts against him. She might not be a real human, but she was a real virgin, and that was more important. He was in a manner falling in love with her, odd as that might seem to anyone who didn't understand about unicorns and virgins.

Take me.

Could he do that in this shared daydream? He wasn't sure. Would it actually be Veee he took, which was not something either of them wanted? Or if he did complete the act with Ladybug, would it cause her to explode and be lost?

No, and no, she responded. *I went over this with Vee, and she will not touch you that way physically. And I will not explode, because what causes that is the pressure of my own mass in inserted seminal fluid, which can't happen in a virtual mating. I will merely suffer the rapture of your sexual love, and feel your orgasm feminized by Veee. I will be your woman as much as is possible, and that will make me utterly happy.*

They had really worked it out! It might be more dream than reality, but dreams could reflect fundamental desires sometimes better than reality allowed. "Then let's do it," he agreed.

Wetzel!

For a moment he was confused. That was not LadyBug's thought. Then he realized it was the bat. Vanja had flown across to join them. "What is it?"

There's a predator coming. A giant carnivorous tree sloth. We have to move.

"Veee," he said. "LadyBug."

Veee woke. The human form of LadyBug dissipated. In a moment both got the message. Wetzel and LadyBug verified the hungry presence of the sloth zeroing in on them.

Go Away! But the thing was too dull to respond. All it cared about was crunching flesh and bones. Because they were in the tree, Wetzel could not transform to unicorn and stab it. They had no choice but to vacate, as Tod had already done.

Wetzel and Veee scrambled out of the nest. They climbed to a lower branch, ready to jump onto the ground, but halted. There were nocturnal lizard predators there, too many to dissuade either physically or mentally. They had to stay tree-borne.

The bat hovered near. *Up is the only way; we already discovered that. Tod's higher.*

They climbed to a higher branch as the hot breath of the sloth sounded near the nest. But the sloth followed. It was slow moving, but completely competent in the tree, and readily kept pace with them. Now Wetzel read its mind: it was sure of its prey, because this was how it always caught it. Driving it upward until it had nowhere to go, then sweeping it in. Slow but sure.

"We're in trouble," he muttered to Veee.

"I heard. Ladybug has me in the loop. It seems this tree gets narrower as it ascends, and the branches don't intersect with others. At least none sturdy enough to support our weight."

"We'll have to go down, then, and risk the reptiles."

But the moment they reversed course, the sloth moved to cut them off. They could not get by it. Up was their only choice.

They climbed, as they could not afford to wait for it. The sloth followed. Sure enough, the central trunk narrowed, its radiating branches becoming smaller. Tod was already there, stopped by the risk of breaking the thinning stem.

"Well, we have knives," Tod said.

Won't work, Vanja thought. *I checked it. That monster's leather hide is so thick and hairy it's almost invulnerable. Our knives would only annoy it.*

It was LadyBug who got the key idea. *Sometimes we bugs help our hosts. Insects can accomplish things knives can't.*

"My fire ants!" Tod exclaimed.

My mosquitoes, Vanja echoed.

Veee laughed nervously. "My flower flies are harmless."

"As is my scarab," Wetzel said.

No, LadyBug thought. *Flies in the eyes can't be ignored. And I can send thoughts to amplify the pain of the stings. The sloth won't know it's not real damage.*

"Well, now," Tod said. "Let's do it."

All you have to do is ask them. Speak and they will hear your mind.

"Ants," Tod said. "Please sting the sloth. I will welcome you back when you're done." Then, surprised: "I feel their agreement!"

Put your hand to the sloth's nose so they can drop onto it.

Tod reached down close to the sloth, which had come up on the trunk during the dialogue and was ready to strike. Wetzel saw or mentally felt a number of tiny insects drop down. They did not remain on the nose; they scurried across the head, down the neck, and into the body. Where were they going?

Meanwhile the Vanja bat hovered close. It seemed the mosquitoes had no more trouble with her transformations than LadyBug did with Wetzel's. The insects hummed down to surround the furry head.

Veee did not need to reach close. Her flower flies simply flew to the sloth's ugly face.

It did not take long for the sloth to react. It tried to sweep the flies from before its eyes, but they danced about as if flitting from flower to flower and could not be harmed by such sweeps. Meanwhile the mosquitoes found its relatively tender ears, crawling in and feasting. And the ants found another site. Wetzel read its mind and relayed its sensation.

"Ooooo!" Tod exclaimed jubilantly. "They're stinging its ass! And it hurts ten times as much as it should."

Wetzel laughed, and even Veee had to smile. LadyBug was sending enhancement for all the insects' attacks. The sloth's eyes were blinking rapidly to avoid fancied bites by the flies, which it did not know were not the stinging kind. Its ears were itching madly. And its bottom was burning, especially where it counted. It would have trouble for hours if it wanted to defecate.

Before long it gave up the chase in the interest of scratching its ears and trying to rub its posterior against a branch. It slowly descended the trunk, realizing that the upper reaches of the tree had become uncomfortable.

"We have won," Tod said. "Now let's collect our bugs."

Call them back.

They followed the sloth down, collecting bugs as they went. The flower flies and mosquitoes were easy, but the ants had to be picked up from the branches and trunk. All of them helped Tod get them; there were a surprising number, and they did not sting any of the team members. Wetzel got several on his hand and passed them to Tod.

They had, indeed won, thanks to their friends. They had not before fully appreciated the advantages in having insect associates.

The sloth moved on to another tree, satisfied that this one was too awkward to hunt in. The team members returned to their two nests. "Where were we?" Wetzel asked, closing his eyes.

The humanized LadyBug reappeared before him, lovely and gloriously virginal. He held her and kissed her, feeling her delight in being so treated. It was an experience she could have in reality only immediately before her demise, so this had the added thrill of cheating death.

A bed appeared. He guided her to it, laid her on it, and kissed her breasts. This affected her only secondarily, as her species had no breasts; she merely felt his pleasure in the act. Then he entered her, and felt her tense.

"No," he told her. "My seminal fluid is only a few drops, not remotely approaching your body mass. It will not distend you to the bursting point, even in imagination"

True. But she remained tense. She simply could not have sex without the expectation of death, though it was what she desired. *Do it.*

She wanted to be forced, at least to this extent. Could he do it?

Do it she repeated urgently.

He did it. He let his climax come upon him, spurting into her. She felt his orgasm and the ejaculate, then relaxed as she confirmed its insignificant volume. She had no orgasm of her own; that would come only as she literally exploded in the course of real mating. She enjoyed his orgasm instead.

Phenomenal!

She had had the experience of sex. Yet she remained virginal. Wetzel continued kissing her, turned on by it.

I love you.

"I love you too, in my fashion," he said. "The way I can love only a virgin." That was absolutely true.

Then they sank together into sleep. Veee stayed out of it, though she too had received the broadcast of his orgasm. The two of them agreed that they had not had sex, not even dream sex. LadyBug had been the participant.

The following three days they explored the world of Refuge, alert for dinosaurs, sloths, and quakes, and slept in their tree nests. They had learned how to deal with the multiple threats of this planet and how to use their associated insects to good advantage.

LadyBug became a regular dream lover, her tension dissipating with experience, reveling in the romance she could never have on her own. *All too soon this mission will be finished, one way or another, and we will separate,* she explained. *I will revert to my bug self, without much intellect or power or more than the shadow of a memory of my time with you. I want to make the most of my opportunity.*

Veee agreed, and continued to facilitate their vicarious affair. She had strong sympathy for any living thing. That was part of what made her such a good friend, for anyone.

As for Wetzel, he now had his closest approach to his ideal partner, who remained essentially virginal despite having virtual sex. Their relationship surely could not last long, but that virginity compelled and delighted him. He, too, was making the most of his opportunity. If only she wasn't a bug!

On the fourth day they saw the cloud approaching. They were ready. They climbed to the feasible height of the tree, and Vanja as a bat flew up into the fog well before it arrived. She was gone some time, while the cloud kept moving. Had something happened?

Then she reappeared. *Amplify your thoughts!* she thought. *Become beacons so Wizard can locate you. Now!*

Her urgency was contagious. Wetzel and LadyBug extended their telepathy, encompassing the others, making their locations mentally clear.

Whoever first finds the chair, grab it.

Then they were floating up from the tree, into the passing cloud. Tod found the hanging chair and grabbed on. Wetzel and Veee rose on up beside the rope. Soon they emerged from the well, first Veee then Wetzel. They scrambled to the ground as the flotation left them. Vanja hovered, watching the well.

Wizard was collapsed in a chair, unconscious, supported by Pinkie. What was wrong with him?

Two girls were winding Tod up in the chair. He appeared, and grabbed the well wall, jumping to the ground. "What happened?" he demanded.

Vanja transformed to human. "Time!" she said. "Four days

passed for us. Less than one minute passed here. They thought we were still getting ready to explore Refuge."

"Under a minute?" Tod repeated. "Time dilation?"

"I don't know what you call it. But that's what happened. It took us a moment to realize. Then I dived right back down to alert you, and Wizard revved up his magic. We had to act immediately, before the portal cloud drifted too far off the mountain."

"And Wizard is worn out from lifting us," Veee said, understanding. Now Wetzel saw in her mind how Wizard could lift them magically, but it was a tremendous strain on him. That was why Tod had to grab the chair, relieving Wizard of his weight. Wizard might not have been able to complete the lift for all three at once.

Wetzel had not doubted that Wizard had magic power, but he had not seen this type in action before. This was impressive. He knew from the minds of the others that Wizard would recover in a few days. He had certainly come through when needed.

"Does this ruin Refuge for you?" he asked LadyBug. "It would be very difficult for humans to adapt to, because of the time differential."

"Which I calculate at a ratio of about ten thousand to one," Tod said. "Refuge advances ten thousand minutes for one minute here."

That explained the seeming speedup of Vanja's thoughts when she first went out, and her statement that she had flown for fifteen minutes. She had.

No. We can prosper there.

"Then we have indeed found our haven."

Tod and Veee nodded. This aspect was a success despite its surprises.

But it was only half of their mission. They still needed to find a male scarab, and a way to get him safely to Refuge. Which could mean tackling the vicious poachers.

CHAPTER 8: SCARABIA

They put Wizard on Wetzel's unicorn back, and he carried the man back to Pink Pebble Village. They had three days to wait while Wizard recovered. They were bound to need him at full magical strength for the next stage of their mission.

Pinkie braced them when they got there. "We have cooperated with you and helped you find a suitable refuge for the scarabs," she said. "Once you get them there, they will leave our vicinity and we will be out of a job."

"I suppose that is true," Tod said. "You should still guard the portal, however."

"We will do that. But our source of wealth will be gone, with no more scarabs coming to us to die."

"I am not sure what we can do to help in that respect," Tod said. "As you know, our mission is to save the scarabs from extinction, and this we are bound to do if we can."

"We are doing you a significant favor by assisting you in your mission. We feel that a return favor is warranted."

Wetzel began to fathom what she had in mind, but let Tod handle it his own way.

"We have three days to wait until Wizard recovers," Tod said. "Can we do you that favor in that time?"

"Yes."

"And what is that favor?" Tod was aware that Pinkie feared he would balk, so was being somewhat diffident.

"We are desperate for male company. Specifically, for the purpose of getting babies. We are in a section of the Amoeba where babies are allowed, as there have not been many recently."

"So we have gathered," Tod said carefully. "What do you have in mind?"

"Two men. Six women. One woman a day per man for three days. Attempting to get her pregnant."

"But such a thing can not be guaranteed! If the woman is not fertile at the moment—"

"We will provide fertile women. We believe that the chances are that three of the six can get pregnant"

Tod looked somewhat helplessly at Veee. "Do it," Veee said. "It's a fair exchange. We do need their help."

Tod looked at her shrewdly. "The men guard the access to Scarabia. They will also lose their source of wealth. They may want a similar exchange."

Vanja laughed. "They can't have it. We're not getting pregnant by any of them."

But Veee understood his meaning. "We may have to buy access by having sex with six men."

"If we men have to do it, don't you women too?" Tod asked.

"Damn it!" Veee swore.

Vanja interceded. "I can handle all six, and make them all satisfied. We can make that deal."

Veee flashed her a grateful glance. "Then it can be done."

Pinkie smiled with admiration. "We could use you in our village, to make up with the men."

"How did it go wrong between your two villages?" Tod asked. "I would have thought that you would get along very well, with your common interest in saving the scarabs."

"It was our fault, really. It seemed to us that all they wanted was free sex, and we refused to be used. Had we been smarter at the outset we would have used sex to handle them, making them amenable to our will. Men are easy to manage, being creatures of a single desire. As it was, balked, they turned ugly, and it worsened from there. Now we can't even approach them without risking rape or worse."

Tod turned to Vanja. "When you go to RedBrick, why don't you tell them that the women asked you to negotiate a rapprochement? A new start, let bygones go. That you represent just a passing taste of what contrite PinkPebble offers, if they can come to terms? They should be interested."

Vanja smiled. "Pinkie, tell your girls to hoist up their skirts and sharpen their management skills, because they'll soon have company."

Pinkie smiled, understanding perfectly. "I will. If you send Red, tell him I'll be expecting him personally. He's a handsome brute."

Vanja transformed and flew out of the house. Wetzel was sure it wouldn't be that easy, but it was certainly a start.

Pinkie reoriented on Tod. "You're a savvy leader. You have the touch. Can you handle a virgin?"

"Handle?"

"You turned down Pisa before. Remember the bee girl? She's

ripe, and I think you can't deny her again."

"You can't," Veee agreed. Given her leave, Tod could not refuse. He nodded.

Pinkie turned to Wetzel. "Petula is a friend of Paige, and her wasps won't bother you. You should find her compatible."

"I can handle her," Wetzel agreed.

"I will tend to Wizard," Veee said. "While the rest of you are busy."

Pinkie led the two men outside. The two young women with the bees and the wasps were there. It seemed that Pinkie was no slouch as a leader herself.

Pisa took Tod's hand. "You may have to be firm with me, the first time. But you have to understand that I really do want this." She led him away. She had evidently learned something from her experience with Wetzel.

That left Petula, a sultry black-haired wench. "I'm different from Paige. I want the illusion of romance. I want to be cuddled and stroked and kissed and savored. What do you want?"

"The same," Wetzel said, smiling.

She led him to her comfortable apartment. "Would you like anything to eat?"

He read her mind, and saw that she was trying to put him at ease, thinking he wasn't. She knew this deal had been forged for reasons that had little to do with actual romance, but nevertheless preferred the illusion. She wanted pleasant interaction before they got to the point.

"I am not hungry," he said. "But if it is not too much to ask, how about playing a game of cards?" He had learned that many of the Amoeba residents, having time on their hands, played with cards.

She was surprised and pleased. "I have cards!" She fetched a deck. "What shall we play for?"

"Kisses."

Soon they were playing a card game she called War, which consisted of laying down one card apiece, together, and the higher one captured the lower one. Petula leaned forward to play her cards, and he saw into her marvelously low décolletage. This was exactly what she intended, but it thrilled him anyway, these supposedly accidental peeks into the cleavage of her breasts. When the two cards matched they had a spot war, piling three cards face down on the first ones, then one more face up, and the higher card took them all.

Wetzel won the first war. "Ha!" he said gleefully. "You must pay me one kiss!"

"Oh, darn," she said with mock reluctance. She yielded gracefully enough and it was a very nice kiss.

When another war came, she won. "My turn!" she exulted. "Pay up!"

"Oh, my," he said, barely feigning his own reluctance. This game was fun. He held her and kissed her.

He finally won the game. "You know what that means, wench? You are mine!"

"I am lost," she agreed, lowering her gaze as she slipped out of her clothing.

They adjourned to her bed. He kissed and stroked her, finding her nicely responsive, and in due course completed the act. This was far better than it had been with her friend Paige.

Glorious! That was Ladybug, reveling in his climax.

Then they cleaned up and played another game of War. "Oh, I wish we could keep you here at PinkPebble Village," she said. "You are accommodating my foibles so well it is almost as if you are reading my mind."

He was doing exactly that, but it was not expedient to say so. "I almost wish I could," he agreed.

"Could read my mind, or could stay here?"

"Both." That wasn't actually a lie. "I'm sure your mind is delightful, and a stay at PinkPebble would surely be delightful too. But as you know, I have this thing about virginity."

"I do know," she agreed. "Pisa blames herself."

"It's the way virgins are. If I could stay longer, having time to properly court them, then I could make it with them. But I couldn't settle down with them. That's what I mean: I can't *stay* with a virgin. Because she doesn't remain a virgin."

I do.

You are a constant joy to me, LadyBug, he thought sincerely.

Petula nodded, not being in the mental circuit. "We appreciate your problem. I think Pinkie's working on it."

"Wish her luck," he said without hope. "It's an unkind paradox."

They continued playing, kissing with each war. Petula won the second game. "Aha! Now you are mine! Get on that bed."

I love the way she loves it!

They played far into the night, both enjoying the game almost as much as the sex. If this was typical of the way PinkPebble treated a man, it would indeed be a nice place to settle. But what about when he ran out of their virgins? He would have to move on.

In due course they slept together in both the sexual and literal senses. Petula was so eager to get pregnant that she was almost as demanding as Vanja, and almost as pleasant to be with.

Almost LadyBug agreed.

Petula kissed him fervently when they parted in the morning. "I think we connected," she said, meaning conception.

The second night was with Paula, a blonde dragonfly girl. She was not much for romantic pretense, but did her best to be seductive, and succeeded. The dragonflies hovered, watching the detail of the action. She, too, was pleasant to be with.

There is something to be said for calculated seduction.

The third night was with Pearl, who had moths; her hair was almost nacreous, like pearls or special moth wings. She was a virgin.

"Now don't get nervous," she said soothingly. "Not all virgins are touchy. I am not personally attracted to you, and I wouldn't want to marry you, but I can do this. It's like a business transaction."

"Normally virgins are not at first attracted to me. It's part of my curse."

"But a realistic one can do the necessary with dispatch." Her mind backed her up. She stripped and showed herself off, and she did have conducive equipment, then gracefully accommodated him when he came to her. "I do lack experience; you will have to take the initiative. I promise to accede without balking."

"I appreciate that. I prefer to kiss you first."

"That I can do."

They kissed, and continued from there. She was tense, as the curse made her dislike this, but her discipline overrode it. Possessing her virginity was glorious, and the appeal did not fade immediately, so they were able to do it several times, thrillingly.

With each repetition her aversion diminished, and by morning she was beginning to like it. But by then she was of course no longer virginal. The curse had not lost its force.

"I believe I am getting to like you," she said as they prepared to rejoin the others. "If you should wish to settle down . . ."

"I would have to keep servicing virgins," he reminded her. "You would not like that."

She made a moue. "True."

Too bad, LadyBug thought. *I liked them all, but there was indeed something special about doing that virgin. I wish I could be her.*

"If we find a male, you can be your own virgin."

The intensity of her reaction surprised him. Sex with a male scarab would kill her, but she desperately longed for it. She tried to imagine Wetzel's little liquid efforts as the hint of the huge fire-hose effort of the male, filling her, distending her to the bursting point so that she could expire in sheer bliss. But that was beyond her power, and she had to settle for the vicarious driblets.

Wetzel had looked forward to her possible mating and demise with quiet dread, but now he realized that it was indeed her fulfillment. He wanted her to achieve it.

Thank you.

Wizard was now recovered enough to travel. It was time to go to Scarabia and search for a male scarab.

"One other thing," Pinkie said.

"You are not satisfied?" Tod asked cautiously.

"I am satisfied with the deal we made. But I would like to know how it turned out. Please, have Wizard scry my girls to see which of them are pregnant."

They all laughed. It made so much sense!

Scrying was one of the less demanding magics Wizard could do. They brought the six girls in to him one by one, and he confirmed that one of Tod's, the virgin, was pregnant. And that all three of Wetzel's girls were pregnant too. They were overjoyed. Their effort of having sex with the two men during their most fertile days was paying off.

"We have simply got to have you with us," Pinkie said to Wetzel. "I'd love to have you in my bed for a night, too." Though she was older, no slender filly, and no virgin, she was breedable and he saw in her mind that she well knew how to please a man. She had a naughty dream of him coming to her wordlessly, throwing her on the bed, and forcefully penetrating her and injecting his seed. The notion turned her on so strongly that the mere thought came close to giving her an orgasm. "I would surely enjoy that," he said politely, and it was the truth. Rough sex could be fun when both parties wanted it that way.

"We're looking for an offer you can't refuse." She was serious, but as yet had no such offer in mind. Obviously she couldn't provide for his ultimate need: a perpetual breedable virgin. He doubted anyone could, though he still foolishly hoped.

"Good luck."

They moved on to the men's village of RedBrick. Tod and Veee walked ahead, holding hands, and Wetzel in unicorn form carried Wizard.

"I fear severe complications," Wizard remarked as he rode. "We will have to leave the Amoeba, and that is bound to be mischief."

"Your magic will work outside?"

"Oh, yes. That's not the problem. It's that the Amoeba is a protected environment. When we leave it we can be separated, hurt, or killed. You saw how it was on Refuge."

"I did."

"And we are likely to encounter poachers. These may be utterly vicious men who will not hesitate to kill anyone who tries to interfere with their criminal business. Your telepathy and my magic should help considerably, but it is still no easy business. The women especially will be at risk."

"They will be," Wetzel agreed. "Vanja can handle it or escape it."

"Actually so can Veee. She has been involuntarily taken by many men in the past. She may handle that better than the prospect of voluntarily doing it with any man other than Tod. It is emotional fidelity she is trying to give him, more than physical. Still, it will be better to avoid such ugliness if at all possible."

This is true. Veee lent me her human female outlook so I could have vicarious sex with you, but that was me, not her. She likes you but does not want sex with you. Because that would be voluntary, and she might really like it, and that would make her be emotionally untrue to Tod.

Exactly. It was the same reason he did not want to have sex with Veee, pleasant as it might otherwise be. They could be true friends only as long as it remained platonic. Her virginity with respect to him made her a better friend.

Wetzel thought of something else. "Assuming we find a male scarab, how can we get it safely through the Amoeba and to Refuge? I understand male scarabs can't survive here."

"I have pondered that during my recovery. I even did a private scry I think is valid. I can't scry the Amoeba itself directly, but I can pose spot questions and come up with likely answers. I gather that there is a certain ambiance the Amoeba maintains, to keep things compatible for occupants of any kind, including atmosphere, gravity, language, and reproduction—"

"Reproduction!"

"Populations are stable here. People can breed only so long as there is local room for them. Part of the suppressive aura affects the men, and part the women. The longer a person remains within the Amoeba, the more he or she is affected. The women of PinkPebble can breed because they have not come close to filling their allotment. If they are able to resume breeding, in due course they will complete that allotment, and then no more babies will be conceived regardless how often they have sex."

"No wonder they are so eager to be the first!"

"Yes. But they will not have to be concerned about that this year or next. One reason you and Tod are so appealing is that you have not spent your lives within the Amoeba, so your fertility remains strong. But that suppressive aura affects the male scarab, who has not a little seminal fluid but a lot. What is a trace effect to a human male, who is constantly expelling ejaculate and generating new semen, is significant to the scarab, who takes a year to build it up. One-fifth to one-quarter of his body mass, in fact. His own fluid will heat and boil and destroy him. So he can't be exposed to that aura, not even for a little while. He will have to be shielded from it."

Yes, he must, LadyBug thought with horror.

"How can he be shielded?"

"This may be where you come in, Wetzel. It seems that a sufficient mass of flesh can damp down the aura, at least for a few hours. A human man wears much of his reproductive equipment outside his body, ready prey to the aura. A woman's equipment is mostly internal, so is better shielded. So most women can conceive with fresh males if the allotment allows it. The need is to put the male scarab into a massive living body, to shield it for the trip through the Amoeba."

"You are thinking of my unicorn form!"

"That may indeed be the reason you were selected for this mission. Your mass."

Wetzel chuckled. "I was warned that the Amoeba's reasons for choosing people are not necessarily complimentary to those people."

Wizard shrugged. "It is merely a conjecture."

"Confirmed by scrying."

"Sometimes I misinterpret a scry."

"How would I put a scarab inside me?"

"He could be put into a capsule which you could then swallow."

"Wouldn't the beetle suffocate?"

"I have learned that they can go into temporary stasis, and survive on very little air for weeks if they need to."

"How would I get it out again?"

"It would emerge on its own, in the normal course."

"As a turd!"

Wizard shrugged. "Perhaps you have a better idea."

Unfortunately Wetzel didn't. He dropped the subject.

We bugs are not as wary of turds as you fleshly folk are. They can be nutritious. Some of our related species, the dung beetles, use them as sustenance for their young.

"I appreciate your encouragement," Wetzel muttered.

"Something else," Tod said. "When Veee visited my frame, not only was she ghostly, but her language was completely foreign. How will we be able to communicate with anyone there?"

"This, too, I have pondered," Wizard said. "There are a myriad languages in the worlds and times and alternate universes, with no single compromise language available, not even sign language. We shall have to use cards."

Cards? Wetzel thought of the games he had been playing.

"Picture cards," Veee said, understanding better than Wetzel did. "I will draw a number of stick figure examples."

"We'll need a reusable tablet too," Wizard said.

"Such things should exist at RedBrick Village," Tod said. "Vanja can do some wheedling."

They arrived at RedBrick Village, where Vanja was just wrapping up. "That is some damsel you have," Red said appreciatively as Wizard dismounted and Wetzel reverted to manform. "She not only did the whole village, she brought news of possible rapprochement with the women of PinkPebble. It seems they are willing to exchange sex for babies."

Vanja had done the whole village? There were about seventy men there. She must have done a man an hour for three days and nights! "She's a capable woman," Tod said, keeping a straight face.

"We would like to have her settle down here. We would treat her very well. We have developed a real taste for vampires."

The bat flew to join Wetzel. *Would you believe, I'm tired of sex? Some of those men wanted it several times in their hour.* Wetzel believed it.

"That would of course be her decision to make," Tod said. "But at the moment we have a mission to complete, and we need her for that."

But after a few minutes rest, I should be back to normal. I trust those Pebble women didn't wear you out?

"They want me to stay, too," Wetzel subvocalized. "I got three pregnant."

Oooo, you bad boy! she thought appreciatively.

"We are ready to use the access to Scarabia," Tod told Red. "You folk having no objection."

"None at all," Red agreed jovially. "Your vampire wench saw to that. Did you know she can nip a man and make him immediately potent again?"

"Yes," Tod said. "That is one of her talents." Wetzel was not telling that Vanja could also nip to make a man forget he had ever had sex with her. Obviously she had not done that with these men.

They rested for an hour, while Vanja wheedled in her fashion. Soon two men were doubly happy, and the team had a thick packet of stiff papers for Veee to draw on, and two erasable tablets. Veee was already busy sketching.

The portal to Scarabia was hidden not far from the village, masked as a deserted cave. "None of us have been there," Red said. "The trail was made by and for the scarabs. The poachers can't use it, if they even know it exists."

"Are scarabs still coming through?" Tod asked.

"Not any more. The poachers have thinned them out so badly that all they do now is hide. You may have trouble finding any."

"We'll manage," Tod said, not mentioning LadyBug or the telepathy.

Vanja flew to the ground and transformed to human form. "Meanwhile why don't you go to PinkPebble and verify what I have told you about rapprochement? You won't need me any more."

"None of those Pebble women match you, vamp."

"But some are young and pretty and eager to get pregnant."

"We'll check it out," Red agreed, obviously interested.

"One other thing," Wetzel said. "Do you have a capsule that will hold a male scarab?"

Red was taken aback. "A capsule? Why?"

"To transport him," Wizard said. "Shielded from the ambiance of the Amoeba by the massive flesh of a unicorn."

Red nodded. "Wow! Let's hope it works." In a moment he produced exactly such a capsule, consisting of two translucent halves that fitted together. "We had thought of transport, but not of shielding."

"Thank you," Wizard said, taking the capsule.

"You may want these to feel your way," Red said, presenting them with staffs. Tod and Veee accepted them; the others did not.

Wetzel transformed back to unicorn, Wizard mounted him, and they proceeded into the cave. It was dark, so Vanja returned to bat form, perched on Wizard's shoulder, and used her echolocation to probe the route ahead.

It's a Trail, she reported mentally to Wetzel. "Good footing, plenty of room, no nasty surprises. Just march on through."

Wetzel relayed her thought. Tod and Veee used their staffs to feel their way and walked with reasonable confidence. That was the advantage of working as a team: they knew they could trust what their members said.

Before long there was light ahead. They came into a lush green world. This was Scarabia, orbiting giant Betelgeuse, origin of the scarabs.

Home!

You have been here? Wetzel thought.

No. But I'd know it anywhere.

They emerged from the end of the trail. The air was warm and sweet, gravity comfortable; it was an Earth-type planet. Wizard dismounted, Wetzel and Vanja transformed to human, and they all stood there appreciating it.

"Why aren't we ghosts?" Vanja asked.

"This is a mission for the Amoeba," Wizard said. "It has the power to extend its ambiance somewhat, at need. It is extending it to us, to enable us to relate to this world in the manner natives would. Otherwise we would not be able to carry the male scarab."

"Then let's find it and get out of here," Vanja said. "I don't want to stay long."

It is the Go Away projection of the scarabs, LadyBug explained. *To which the poachers are unfortunately immune.*

Wetzel relayed that. "So there are scarabs still here," Tod said.

Yes. Hiding. But they are coming out of hiding. Oh, my! Her expressions mimicked those of the humans, as it was a human mind that was amplifying her own mind.

"What is it?"

There's a male! And he is approaching mating time. I must go to him.

"There's a male!" Wetzel repeated for the others. "LadyBug is attracted."

"This is too easy," Vanja said.

"Scry it," Tod told Wizard.

Wizard stood, concentrating. "There are scarabs, many females, one male, the females attracted to the male. In a few more days he will be ready to breed. But there is something wrong. Danger. I can't define it further without getting closer to its source."

"I can," Tod said. "Poachers."

"Maybe we can verify that," Wetzel said. "LadyBug feels the male; can you scry the connection?"

"Perhaps I can, if I can borrow her," Wizard said.

"Your spider—will she be safe from that?" For Wizard carried the deadly brown recluse spider. Wetzel wasn't sure what it preyed on.

"It will not prey on any of the insects of this party," Wizard assured him.

True.

Wetzel approached Wizard. LadyBug flew across to him, and Wizard did another scry.

"The male is captive of the poachers," Wizard said. "They know it is becoming breedable and will attract females. They are using it to bring them in so they can have a record haul."

"The monsters!" Vanja said. "They are hastening the extinction!"

"We shall have to rescue that male," Tod said. "But if the poachers are like those of my world, and I believe they are, they will be utterly vicious men. The women will not be safe from rape, or the men from torture and murder."

"We shall have to deceive them long enough to get that male," Vanja said. "Then all bets are off."

"How?" Veee asked.

"Perhaps we could become an entertainment group," Wizard said. "I could tell an engaging story, Vanja can dance, Tod can play his pipe, Veee can set the stage."

"What of me?" Wetzel asked. "My art is drama; I can act a part. But not in my unicorn form, as I will have to be to transport that male scarab."

"You can be the unicorn summoned by virgins," Veee said, smiling.

"There is something else," Tod said. "Assuming we get close, and find the male, and get him in the capsule and all, those Poachers are not going to simply let us walk away. We need an escape plan."

Wetzel picked up a worry in Wizard's mind. He could foil pursuit via illusion, but this was a new planet and he hadn't tried it here. He did not want to alarm the others needlessly, but he wanted a pretext to test it in this venue.

So Wetzel set it up for him. "Maybe if we could somehow fool them, lead them astray?"

"I may be of use here," Wizard said, his mind appreciating Wetzel's effort. "My cheapest yet most effective magic is illusion. The poachers will not be able to pursue us far through that."

"I don't mean to question your competence," Wetzel said. "But why wouldn't the poachers simply ignore the illusion and follow us?"

Wizard smiled. "Perhaps a small demonstration will suffice. Let's say our path runs beside a dangerous drop-off. There to our left." He gestured, and the drop appeared, with a path beside it to the right. "We know the route, but the poachers don't. We run along it, but what they, following moments later, see is this." The path and drop switched places.

Wetzel nodded, remembering Wizard's prior demonstration, which the other members of the team had not seen him make for Wetzel. Both path and drop looked completely realistic. The pursuers would take the path without thinking, especially if the fleeing folk were just in sight beyond a curve. They would plunge into the drop. If they didn't die, they would at least be slowed. Thereafter they would not dare charge at speed, and would lose the team. "It will do," he agreed. It was a reminder that illusion could be most dangerous by covering up a real threat, instead of making a fake one. And Wizard was now reassured that his powers worked on Scarabia.

Thank you, Wizard's thought came. Wetzel just smiled.

You're a nice man, LadyBug thought.

"Anything to impress a virgin," he subvocalized.

"Now the ensemble," Tod said. "We need to rehearse it, if we are to be effective."

"I will tell a tale of a pretty girl who hears lovely music, follows it, and discovers a dancing nymph," Wizard said. "The nymph asks if she is a virgin, and when she confirms it, the nymph tells her of a local unicorn that needs to be tamed. So the girl goes to the unicorn, and he lies down and puts his head in her lap, and she is able to catch him and tame him. Will that suffice?"

"What does she do with him once she has him?" Tod asked.

Wizard frowned. "The stories I have heard conclude with the death of the unicorn. We don't want that in this case. Maybe she trains him as a steed. He can walk around, carrying her, incidentally searching out a male scarab."

"There's another problem," Vanja said. "Even if we convince the poachers we're an ensemble, they're not likely to respect our persons any better than they respect the scarabs or the law. How can we be safe from them?"

"We need to be a step ahead of them," Wizard said. "Wetzel's telepathy will help. We can get close enough to read their minds, then decide our course."

Veee looked at Tod. "Have your gun ready." And at Wizard. "And your bomb. We girls will have our knives. We may have to kill some men before we get clear of this with the male scarab. An appeal to their decency won't work."

"We may indeed," Wizard agreed. "Perhaps it would be better to appeal to their greed. We can mention that we know where a hidden cache of scarabs is."

"Won't work," Vanja said. "They'll know it can't be anything local, and we don't want them to know about the Amoeba."

"Then what do you suggest?" Wizard asked her sharply.

"We're a party from a client planet that's been paying through the nose for scarabs. We want to cut out the middleman and deal directly with the source. Our employers have whatever money they need; they just don't like overpaying. This will suggest that the poachers can get more money by dealing with us directly. They'll like that. But we'll be canny about our planet, for obviously reasons; not of this trade is legal. So we pose as an ensemble so our traveling will seem innocuous."

"You have a criminal mind, wench!" Wizard said.

"Thank you." She flashed her fangs at him.

They refined the details. Then Wetzel turned unicorn, Wizard mounted, Vanja made a brief bat flight and then joined them, and they moved slowly toward the male scarab.

"PS, LadyBug," Wizard said. "I know you are desperate to connect with that male, but we need you a while longer. You must hold back until we actually rescue him and get him to Refuge. If you go to him before then, all will be lost."

I understand, LadyBug responded as she returned to Wetzel. *I will restrain myself. Anyway, he's not yet quite ready to breed; it will be a few more days.*

The landscape was beautiful. It was hilly and rocky, and there were indeed gulfs between trees, as if flooding rivers had cut through and gouged out sections. "Illusion masking these could be quite effective," Wizard said.

"It's not enough," Tod said. "The first one who drops into a gulf will alert the others and they'll pull up short."

"We need something that will already be too late by the time they catch on," Veee said.

"That's a difficult order," Wizard said.

"All it takes is a quicksand bog overlaid by floating debris," Vanja said. "Run out over it, it starts to sink, back off, but you're already going down."

"And do you have such a bog handy?"

"Scry for it, dodo."

"I'm not sure a scry of that nature would work."

"Stop balking, or I'll kiss you."

"You don't understand. Scrying is local. I could scry the nature of a bog if I came to it, but—"

Vanja changed to bat form, flew to land on Wetzel's back in front of Wizard, transformed to nude woman form, soundly kissed him, transformed to bat, flew to the ground, and returned to woman. "Scry the local land."

Wizard sighed. "Your argument is persuasive."

The others laughed as Wizard dismounted and stood directly on the land. He looked surprised. "We are on a slope that descends to a bog."

Vanja looked smug. She had seen the lay of the land during her flight.

They soon found the bog, and it was indeed quicksand. "But we'll have to lead them to it," Tod said. "If it is concealed by illusion, how will we avoid it ourselves?"

Veee studied the bog. "We will have to skirt it carefully, as the outline is curvaceous. We have to be able to see it."

"Curvaceous outlines are made to be seen," Vanja agreed, flexing her hips.

"I shall have to teach you to penetrate illusion," Wizard said. "Then you will be able to navigate it safely, while the poachers won't."

"Now," Tod said.

Wizard dismounted again, and Wetzel reverted to manform. Wizard cast an illusion of rocky hills and gullies much like those they had been traversing. It was so realistic that Wetzel hesitated to move at all, lest he put a foot into quicksand.

"The key is first to know that you face illusion," Wizard said. "Second, to know the underlying reality. Focus on that reality until it begins to come clear beneath the fog of illusion. Remain focused until you are through it."

"Couldn't the poachers do that too?" Veee asked.

"They could if they knew how, if they anticipated the ploy. We are depending on the element of surprise."

Wetzel focused on the bog he had just seen, that he knew was there. Gradually the illusion thinned, like fog he was seeing through, and the bog achieved increasing solidity. When he refocused on the illusion, it was back in force, but it was easy now to return to the bog. He stepped forward and touched the edge of the bog with his toe. It was definitely a marsh.

Fascinating, LadyBug thought. *I can do illusion to make my body resemble a flower fly, but Wizard can mask an entire landscape.*

"That's his specialty," Wetzel said. "It's a form of magic."

You call it that because you don't know how he does it.

She had a point. In some cultures Wizard would be called a scientist or an artist.

The others were doing likewise, getting their bearings despite the cover of illusion. Once they all had it straight, Wizard let the illusion lapse. Tod with Vanja in bat form explored the land between the bog and the access to the Amoeba trail, planning a route. Wetzel and Veee explored in the direction of the male scarab, on whom LadyBug had a firm fix.

Yet why hadn't Veee gone with Tod? They were in love, after all.

Veee smiled. "I caught that."

Wetzel was embarrassed. "I keep forgetting that LadyBug enables me to project my thoughts."

I do.

"It's no matter," Veee said. "We separate *because* we are in love. When we are alone together the temptation to make love is too great, and whatever other business we are about suffers."

"But Vanja will be seducing him."

"Of course. That's her nature. But that's sex, not love. Not nearly as much of a distraction. She can accomplish it in minutes and go on about their business. He retains a lingering hankering for her."

"You are remarkably tolerant."

"Tolerant of him with her. Of him with the girls of PinkPebble. Intolerant of my being sexual with any other man."

"I don't properly understand that. If it is all right for him to have sex with other women, why isn't it all right for you to have sex with other men?"

"Tod would allow it. He is not jealous. But I came from a primitive culture where women have no sexual rights. Now I am in one where they do. I am reserving myself for Tod alone. This is my expression of personal privilege."

"Vanja suggested something similar. She supports your resolution."

"She does. We are friends."

The male scarab is close.

"We had better halt here," Wetzel said. "The male scarab is near."

"I heard. Now we have a route from here to the bog."

They started back, mentally marking the route. "I hope our plan is effective," Wetzel said.

"So do I. I fear for the future."

"You have precognition?"

"No, just common sense. We know the poachers are brute men. We know what interests men. They will want to possess both Vanja and me. We may be able to get along with them only if we pay in that manner."

"I fear you are right."

Suddenly she was in mental and physical tears. "Oh, Wetzel, I don't want to do it!"

Quite understandable. "We can tell them no."

"Not if we want free rein to search for the male scarab."

I will know exactly where he is.

"But you dare not get close to him," Wetzel said to LadyBug. "One of us must do it, and persuade him to travel with us. The poachers will be on guard against that."

"I am going to have to prostitute myself," Veee sobbed.

Wetzel took her in his arms, trying to comfort her. "We'll work out a different plan."

"We don't have time. We need to get this done today, before that male scarab is ready to breed. Before all the other females flock to him, and get juiced by the poachers."

She is right.

"We'll discuss it today," Wetzel said. "There has to be another way."

"I doubt it. But thanks for trying." She lifted her wet face and kissed him.

It was a friendship kiss, but it electrified him; there were echoes of his love scenes with the dream virgin LadyBug that caught him off guard. "You're welcome," he said somewhat hollowly. He felt guilty for desiring her. They were friends, not lovers.

And of course she got that thought too. Damn his carelessness! He should have buried it.

"No, there must be truth between friends," Veee said. "You desire me and I desire you. I believe I am about to prostitute myself to strange ugly men. I would rather give myself to you before soiling myself that way. You care. You are determined to be my friend despite your sexual interest."

"Yes! So let's have no more of this."

"I am in this respect virginal. I have given myself voluntarily to only one man. You must be the second."

He fought his burgeoning desire. She was right: it was a type of virginity. "No! What you do involuntarily is not your fault. But you must not betray your voluntary code. We must return to the bog now."

"You are struggling," she said. "Dragging yourself one way when your wish is another way."

There was no point in trying to deny it. "I am." He walked back the way they had come.

She followed, grasping his hand. "You are stronger than I am. I love you."

"May I always be worthy of it." He kept moving.

"Thank you." Her overflowing emotions were highly mixed, but the dominant one now was relief.

The others knew the moment they came in range. "You are more of a man than I took you for, unicorn," Wizard said. Both Tod and Vanja nodded.

"We have to figure out another way," Wetzel said. "We can't let

Veee do what repulses her."

"It isn't entirely your choice," Veee said. Her tears were gone; she had made up her mind.

"Yet if we can find an alternative strategy," Wizard said, "then perhaps we can preserve what we value."

"We'll work on it now," Tod said grimly. His mind said he was against letting Veee prostitute herself, but not because of his own interest. Because he didn't want her hurt, and this would mortify her.

Then they felt the feather touch of a telepathic probe. All of them instantly dived into their mental storm shelters, and LadyBug dropped into anonymous repulsion.

But it meant that their mission had just become infinitely more complicated and dangerous. That had been no insect touch; it had the power of a human mind.

The poachers had a telepath among them.

CHAPTER 9: MALEBUG

———

"Verbal communication only," Wetzel said tersely. "With luck they don't realize we have a telepath too."

"What course of action?" Wizard asked. "If we retreat immediately, we can escape them."

"And fail our mission," Vanja said.

"We'll try for it," Tod decided. "Vanja, spy on them. If there are fewer than five, we'll go for it." Vanja transformed and took off. "But have your weapons handy. With a telepath, they will know we're coming. If they attack, we'll treat them like wolfkeys and take down as many as we can." He turned to Wizard. "If all else fails, bomb them, even if you have to bomb us too. At least we'll take them out with us, and save some scarabs."

Wetzel changed to unicorn form so Wizard could ride. He now appreciated how the man had to save his magical power for emergency use. It could make a real difference.

"And if we get the scarab, flee," Tod added. "Along this path, with the illusion."

They all knew why.

The bat returned and transformed to the woman. "Four. Three men and a woman. They have a similar look about them; I think they are siblings."

"That makes sense," Wizard said. "A family affair. They can trust each other."

"We can handle four," Tod said grimly. "Remember, we're a troupe."

"A fake troupe," Vanja said. "To cover our identity as buyers."

"Take this," Veee said, extending the scarab capsule. Wetzel took it in his mouth, tucking it into a cheek.

As they approached the camp of the poachers, Wetzel felt the mental touch again, and knew that the others did too. None of them reacted; ordinary people generally did not know of telepaths, or how to protect their minds. They would keep their assumed identities uppermost in their thoughts, so that these alone could be read. Wetzel himself focused on simply being a unicorn being used as a beast of burden. With luck the telepath would not catch on that he had human intelligence, let alone telepathy. With enough luck, the poachers would not catch on to anything until it was too late.

LadyBug, nestled in the hair of his head, remained silent, knowing that discovery could mean her death.

No poacher came out to meet them. That meant that the poachers were playing dumb, pretending to be unaware of the party's approach. That meant in turn that the poachers were also concealing their telepath. So probably they did not know the visitors had a telepath, let alone which one of them it was. Unless they were being really canny. The dangerous game was on.

"Hello!" Tod called as they sighted the camp.

The poachers jumped up as if surprised. Knives appeared.

Tod spread his open hands in a signal of nonaggression. "Are you the traders?" he asked innocently. "Traders" was a phenomenal euphemism.

The four stared blankly at him. Answer enough; there was no common language.

Veee brought out her cards. "We come as friends," she said, showing a picture of a stick figure man with arms spread in welcome. "I am Veee." She showed a stick figure in a skirt, with long hair.

The woman came forward. "Zora," she said. She had short black hair and a prominent chin, as did the men.

"Hello Zora!" Communication had been, if not established, initiated. Wetzel could have read their minds independent of language, but that would have given away his ability to their telepath.

The two women entered a pictures/words dialogue, in the course of which introductions were made: Tod, Wizard, Vanja, and the unicorn steed Wetzel, presented as a dumb animal. The poachers were Frank, Ralph, and Mason. Wizard and Tod sat on the ground, letting Veee carry it. Vanja stood a little apart, looking bored. Wetzel knew she wasn't, but she wanted to seem like an empty-headed dance girl.

Veee attempted business. She showed a distant planet the team supposedly represented, and a picture of a scarab. That got the immediate and hostile attention of all four. For all they knew, this was really a vigilante posse out to get them. Veee made the case that they wanted to buy scarabs directly, to save money, but none of the poachers trusted that.

Still, the poachers were clearly keenly interested in money, and were not about to dismiss a chance for it out of hand. "We'll talk further tomorrow," Zora said via a card showing the sun going down, then coming up again. "Now show your good faith by entertaining us." That took a number of cards.

Tod brought out his ocarina, and Vanja danced. The music was lovely, and the dance was erotic. The men watched that briefly, then decided they wanted more of her. They took off their clothes and let their erections show. That was clear enough. Would she accede voluntarily? This was a likely crisis point: if the team wanted supposedly friendly relations to continue, Vanja would have to come to terms with the three men.

Vanja was ready. She went with them into their tent. Wetzel wished he could peek into her willing mind, or theirs, to see exactly what the three were doing with her, simultaneously, but he could not risk it. One of these four was a telepath, and that peek could be known.

Similarly Wetzel should be able to identify the poacher's telepath if he tried a peek. But there was no mental touch. Obviously their telepath was being just as cautious. This was a secondary game being played, and another reason both parties were trying to make nice. Whoever identified the other telepath first would have a significant advantage. If it came to violence, the death of the opposing telepath would enable the surviving one to operate freely.

Tod, Veee, and Wizard resumed their dialogue with Zora, who seemed to be getting increasingly interested in Tod. She was not a really attractive woman, but neither was she a washout. Definitely not a virgin. Her posture was subtly shifting to show more flesh to Tod, to evoke his interest. Zora was not well endowed, but clearly female, and she was indeed becoming interesting to the male eye. She would be making her move soon enough, maybe when her brothers finished with Vanja. The poachers were smart enough to keep at least one of their number alert at all times.

Wetzel, a beast ignored, wandered around, grazing on local brush. Untended animals could get into mischief, but this was a glade in a jungle with nothing to mess up. Nothing but the male scarab, which the poachers had not mentioned. It was definitely the time to explore.

Guided by a faint direction signal LadyBug provided, Wetzel ranged nearer the male scarab. He was in a fine-mesh cage under its own shelter, provided with leaves to feed on. He looked like LadyBug but was larger, several times her mass. He was beautiful, scintillating iridescently. What Tod called the Mandelbrot bug, fuzzing into a kind of infinity at the fringe.

LadyBug was almost wild with desire. She kept her thoughts low, but she was perched on his head and he could feel it by direct contact.

This was a window of opportunity that would soon close as the three men finished with Vanja. Wetzel was sure the vampire was extending the session as much as possible, to give Wetzel more time, but any man's passion was soon satisfied by an obliging woman. Then the men would be out, and the chance would be gone.

Wetzel put his head near the cage. "Tell him," he murmured to LadyBug.

She projected their situation, using her amplified power of Wetzel's mind. The male felt it immediately. Because she was one of his own kind, and mental, and breedable, he knew it was the truth. All he had to decide was whether it was worth the gamble.

Now, with the magnification that Wetzel's ambiance provided, the scarab did some quick thinking and knew that he was doomed the moment his readiness brought in the females. He would be squished for juice when his usefulness as bait was done. He had either to escape, or to trust Wetzel and LadyBug.

Wetzel worked the hinged capsule open with his tongue. Then he used his horn to poke a hole in the wire of the cage. Now the male could fly away if he chose. He did not have to cooperate with them.

The male got on the horn and quickly followed it to Wetzel's nose. He went from there to the mouth. He entered the capsule, which fit him comfortably. He had decided on the greater good.

Wetzel tongued the capsule closed and pressed it tight. Then he swallowed it.

Zora's head snapped around. She made a scream of outrage. She brought out an odd little box. The three men boiled out of the tent, naked.

Wetzel didn't wait. He started walking away, knowing the others would follow and that Vanja would catch up. *I have the male!* he thought.

And we have you! Zora thought. Her language was alien, but her thought was clear. She was the other telepath.

Wetzel broke into a gallop. Zora ran to intercept him, holding the box. Then pain enveloped him. It was like a burning fire baking his head, scorching his eyes, spreading out to his neck and shoulders. He collapsed, unable to walk.

Zora snapped orders to the men. They brought large shackles connected by a chain.

Veee drew her knife. Tod reached for his gun.

Zora swung the box around to cover them. Both dropped to the ground, stricken. Meanwhile the men set the shackles on Wetzel's front legs. Now his legs were chained together, hobbling him. Even in his pain, it occurred to him that this was a mistake on the part of the poachers; they should have hobbled his hind legs so he couldn't kick, or the legs on one side so he couldn't run.

It did not take the poachers long to make their case, regardless of the language barrier: any resistance by any of the team members would bring immediate box pain to Wetzel. He was hostage for their cooperation.

Veee had to give up her knife, and Tod his gun. It seemed that the poachers had encountered guns before, and knew what they were. Now Veee and Tod too were shackled, their hands bound behind them. Wizard and Vanja had not drawn weapons or made hostile moves, and were left free. That message, too, was plain enough.

Now the poachers considered Wetzel. Frank made a lifting signal with his hands, and when Wetzel did not respond right away, Frank kicked him on the shoulder. Wetzel struggled to get to his feet, precariously balancing on his linked front hoofs.

The four consulted in their opaque language. Wetzel could have picked up their thoughts telepathically, as telepathy was largely independent of surface language, but refrained. He now knew what Zora was their telepath, but wasn't sure she knew he was the team's telepath. Why would it be a beast instead of a human? Any use of it at this time would give him away immediately. With luck the poachers figured him for a dumb animal trained to swallow scarabs, a neat way to smuggle them past planetary authorities. She should not know that he had human intelligence, or indeed that he was a shape changer. He kept those items buried in his storm shelter. She could read his superficial mind, which he carefully kept basic: serve man, avoid pain.

Another thing the poachers didn't know about was their assorted bugs. Certainly they did not know that Wetzel carried a female scarab masked as a ladybug. Zora had been tracking the male scarab telepathically, and knew the instant the scarab entered the fleshly shielding of Wetzel's body, dimming his access. But that might be most of what she knew. The poachers should figure that the team was looking for scarabs, but that rather than pay for them it proposed to steal them. That would make perfect sense to poachers, who were thieves themselves.

After a brief dialog, Ralph went to the tent and returned with a bag of oats. He sat that down before Wetzel. "Gronk!" he commanded.

Wetzel put his nose down and took a mouthful of oats. Now he understood their strategy: feed him until his digestive process carried the capsule out the other end and they could recover the scarab. That would take about two days. Thereafter they could resume their prior strategy. All they had to do was wait.

Now the poachers considered Tod and Veee. This was exactly what Veee had feared. Mason grabbed Veee's shoulder, evidently interested in new female flesh, and started to open her shirt to expose her bosom, but Zora snapped a demurral. Wetzel could guess its nature: You men had your fun with the sexy wench. Now it's my turn. You don't get the other woman until I've had mine with the man. Your turn for guard duty, you slackers.

Grumbling, the three men acceded. Zora caught Tod's shoulder and tugged him forward.

He balked.

Zora spoke to the men. Frank picked up the pain box. He oriented it on Wetzel.

"Okay, okay," Tod said. Wetzel could understand him because of the extended Amoeba ambiance that applied to the team. Otherwise Tod too would have been rendered verbally unintelligible. He stepped forward.

Zora nodded. She had made her point. Tod would behave. He would have to perform with his hands tied behind him, but he *would* perform. She guided him to the tent.

Meanwhile the three poacher men gazed on Vanja, who gazed

back, and Veee, who did not. They talked among themselves, evidently comparing the visible qualities of the two women. Now that Zora was not watching, Mason went again to draw aside Veee's shirt. He opened it wide, so that both breasts showed clearly.

There was an exclamation from the tent. Mason's hand snapped away. Zora was watching telepathically.

Still, now the three men had a solid basis for comparison. They looked back and forth between the two woman, making comments. Vanja was amused; Veee wasn't.

There was another outcry from the tent. This time Zora emerged in dishabille, furiously scratching herself. She had burning red welts on her bottom. It seemed she had encountered a nest of fire ants.

Vanja and Veee kept straight faces. Tod's insect friends had struck.

Compelled by Zora, the three men got to work beating the ground around and inside the tent. Then they took down the tent and moved it to another site. There was no further sign of ants. Evidently it had been a fluke.

Now Wetzel noticed something about the three men. All were absentmindedly scratching. It seemed that they had recently encountered a swarm of mosquitoes, and been thoroughly bitten while distracted. Vanja's mosquitoes. The mere touch of Wetzel's horn could have ameliorated all their itches, but it seemed they didn't know about unicorns, and the team would not tell them.

Zora put salve on her welts. It seemed she had not gotten satisfaction from Tod before getting stung. The coincidence of the occurrence had turned her off Tod, but she remained determined to have her turn. She eyed Wizard.

But the day was late, so the poachers let that be. They raided the team's packs, rousting out food for the evening meal, and shared it with their captives. After all, they had time to pass, and they wanted the two women handy, and perhaps also the two men.

As night fell, the poachers set up turns for guard duty. Tod and Veee were told by gestures to sleep on the ground and not try to escape, because Zora was tracking them. Zora held the pain box and stayed near Wetzel while Frank took Vanja into the tent. It seemed that Vanja was still allowed; it was Veee who had to wait on Zora's satisfaction. That was the poacher's compromise.

An hour later Frank emerged and Ralph went in. An hour after that Mason went in. Vanja was giving them all excellent service, but somehow they were scratching worse than ever.

Then Frank took the pain box and Zora took the tent, alone. Ralph and Mason made hay mats on the ground and slept on them. After an hour Frank passed the box along to Ralph and settle for sleep himself. They were thieves and rapists, but they had discipline where it counted; they never stopped watching Wetzel and the team members.

Meanwhile Wetzel's oats were coursing through his system. He knew that in hours he would have to defecate out that capsule. He would have to escape before then.

In the morning, after breakfast, Zora decided: it was time for Wizard. The men had been getting increasingly impatient for access to Veee, so Zora had to act. Her ant welts had subsided after giving her a night of pain. She was not in a good mood. She took Wizard into the tent.

Would Wizard use his brown recluse spider? Its bite was said to be severe, sometimes lethal. Or would he prefer to wait?

There was an exclamation from the tent. Zora emerged again, this time rubbing her neck. There was a pinpoint sore there, rapidly becoming a welt. Then she dropped to her knees.

The men rushed to her, but were not able to help her. She collapsed unconscious.

She had been bitten by the brown recluse spider, and was having a serious reaction.

With the telepath out for the time being, Wetzel was free to use his own telepathy. That brought bad news.

The three brothers were concerned for their sister, but not to the point of serious alarm. They were discussing using the temporary reprieve from her authority to rape Veee. Zora had after all had her chance at the men.

Worse, if Zora did not recover soon, they would know this mission was jinxed and wrap it up immediately. They would kill their captives, slaughter the unicorn and cut out the capsule containing the scarab.

The team members could stop this, but only by giving away their other abilities. So they waited.

First the poachers tied Tod's manacled hands to a tree so that he could not interfere. They used ordinary cord to tie Vanja similarly, not trusting her to stay clear. Then Frank grabbed Veee from behind. Ralph dragged down her pants. She tried to kick him, but Mason grabbed her legs. Vanja seemed uncertain. She could escape her bonds and intercede, but only by giving away her nature.

Wetzel did not need to see more. He transformed to human, slipped the shackles off his suddenly thinned wrists, and transformed back immediately. He was free, unobserved, and still a unicorn. It had never occurred to the poachers that he could be a shape changer.

He ran to the tent, where Wizard was just emerging. *Mount!* Wetzel projected. Wizard scrambled on.

Frank and Ralph had Veee bare, her breasts heaving with her struggles, her legs held well apart. Mason was dropping his own pants.

Vanja, guided by Wetzel's example, transformed to bat, readily slipped her bonds, and reverted to human form so rapidly that the poachers would not know what happened unless they were looking directly at her. They weren't. So they did not know her secret either. They were focused on Veee as Mason closed on her, ducking down to come up between her spread legs. They were all turned on.

"Ho, varlets!" Wizard called.

Frank turned his head to look. He gaped. Then the other two looked. All three men were belatedly catching on that somehow the unicorn had slipped his bonds. Frank let go of Veee and dived for the pain box, but Vanja got there first. She swooped it up and aimed it at the men. They gaped at her too.

Nothing happened. She didn't know how to turn it on. Annoyed, she hurled it into the brush.

"Get the gun!" Wizard called. "Get the knife!"

Vanja knew exactly where they were. She fetched them while Wetzel menaced the poachers with his horn. That was no bluff; he could readily kill the first one to make a hostile move.

Meanwhile Veee recovered her pants and managed to work them on by leaning her back against a tree trunk for balance while she held them behind her feet. It was clumsy, but worked. Wetzel noticed in passing how she had not freaked out or dissolved into tears; she had kept her head and acted the moment she could. Neither had Tod bothered with pointless protests or threats; he had seen Wetzel and Vanja acting, and waited on their help. Nervy people, all.

Vanja went to Tod and in moments untied him from the tree. She couldn't free him of the shackles, but at least now he could move.

"Run!" Tod said to Veee. The two of them ran, hands still bound behind their backs. Vanja followed with the weapons.

Once the others were clear, Wetzel could follow them. He eyed the poachers. *Kill them?* he asked Wizard.

"There is no need," Wizard replied. "We're not murderers, and they're just one fragment of an ugly swarm of thieves. We can't do anything about the larger problem. We've got what we came for. Leave them behind. They've got enough of a problem with Zora, who will probably require medical care."

Wetzel was relieved. He could kill, and had done so before, but he didn't like it. He turned and galloped after the others.

In moments he caught up. Tod and Veee had slowed to a walk, as running with their hands behind them was wearing.

Vanja returned Veee's knife to her, sheathing it in a pouch hidden in her pants. Then she fitted Tod's gun into a holster on his back. They still couldn't use their weapons, but at least they had recovered them.

"Keep moving," Wizard called. "I foolishly spared the poachers, and they may come after us." He wasn't blaming Wetzel for their joint decision.

The poachers did indeed pursue them. Wetzel realized why: they wanted the male scarab. Greed overwhelmed any fear they might have, and they still didn't know how Wetzel and Vanja had freed themselves. They had no gratitude for being spared, merely contempt for the lack of nerve displayed.

Vanja changed and flew back. Soon she had a report: *They are gaining rapidly. They'll catch us before we reach the trail.*

Wizard smiled. "We are prepared. Remember your illusion penetrating technique."

They came to the quicksand bog. Then it disappeared, becoming more rocky hills, as before.

Could you simply make us invisible? Wetzel thought.

"Not readily. The scene is a set piece. We are moving targets I would have to fix on individually. I would lose control over the other illusion."

They focused, and the bog became apparent. They made their way around it, carefully, not hurrying. They needed to know exactly where they put each foot.

The three poachers caught up to the brink of the bog. They saw the fleeing party not far ahead. With a cry of victory they plunged on.

Into the bog. All three of them.

Wetzel looked back. He saw the three men floundering in the seemingly solid ground. The illusion did not cover them, just the land. It was weird.

He put his foot down on a stone, and his ankle turned. Pain shot up his leg, and he almost fell before he caught himself and balanced on the three other legs. Oh, no!

The others, alerted by the flash of pain in his mind, closed in around him. "You can't walk on that," Vanja said. "Can you change to human form so you can use just your hind legs?"

No. That would not shield the male scarab sufficiently when we traverse the Amoeba.

"Ouch."

"Can you use your horn to heal yourself?" Veee asked.

No. I can heal others, not myself.

"Wizard?" Veee asked.

"I could help, but only if I let the illusion lapse."

"That's not yet safe," Tod said.

MaleBug is almost ready to mate, LadyBug reported. *I feel his growing urgency. Oh, I want to be there for him!*

And Wetzel's system was almost ready to pass the capsule out. It would have been timed perfectly, if only he had not been foolishly distracted and hurt himself. Now he could walk only three footed.

"MaleBug? Vanja asked. "Maybe that does make sense."

Wizard dismounted. "Magic is not always the answer. We need a splint."

They foraged and found suitable sections of wood. Wizard and Vanja worked together to fashion the splint and tie it on with cloth from Veee's shirt.

Wetzel tried putting his foot down. It seemed to be able to bear weight, but was still painful.

"I don't like doing this, as it could facilitate injury," Wizard said. "But I will fashion a pain block. That's minimal magic."

The pain faded from the ankle. Now Wetzel could walk normally.

"But be careful," Veee cautioned. "Treat it as if it still hurts."

That was good advice. Wetzel took a few steps, favoring the foot though it no longer hurt. He knew the pain was there, and treated it with respect.

"And I will walk," Wizard said.

"We may need more of your magic," Veee said. "You must save your strength. I will carry you."

Wetzel looked at her with surprise. Was she joking? For one thing, she remained manacled.

Then she stooped, and Wizard draped himself over her shoulder. She straightened up and walked. She was a woman, and her hands were bound, but she was doing the job.

They moved on, not as fast as they would have preferred, but adequately. The poachers, having extricated themselves from the bog, still faced the illusion. They couldn't see to pursue effectively. Maintaining the illusion had been the correct decision.

Then something else happened. Female scarabs appeared, flying in from all around. They came to land on Wetzel.

The breeding! LadyBug thought. *They are aware of the potential, as I am. Oh, I don't want to lose him!*

Wetzel hadn't considered this aspect. *You have been helping us to locate and rescue him. That surely counts for something.*

It does. We have been in touch. MaleBug likes me. He wants to breed me. But if there are others, he has to consider them too. He has to be fair.

There were dozens of scarabs clinging to his coat. Refuge would need a population of mature scarabs. So this was good. But he did feel for LadyBug.

And for himself. *LadyBug, you have been my constant companion these past few days. You enhance my powers. With you, I can send as well as read. You are also a virgin. I love our mock sex sessions! I wish I could keep you with me.*

I wish I could stay with you too. It is wonderful the way you enhance me, and I love being your mock lover. But my destiny is to breed if I possibly can manage it.

Of course, he agreed. *I want you to fulfill your destiny, as I wish I could fulfill mine.* Then he got an idea. *LadyBug, if you go to Refuge with MaleBug, and you breed with him, that's wonderful for you though sad for me. But if he should breed with one of the others, you could return to the Amoeba to be with me again.*

She considered. *I will do that, Wetzel. It is better than dying unfulfilled.*

They reached the Amoeba trail. Wetzel walked toward it.

"Haaa!" it was the verbal and mental cry of victory.

It was Zora. Wetzel read her mind. She had recovered from the spider bite enough to treat herself medically, and then recovered enough strength to go after them herself. Sheer willpower had driven her. The bog illusion was gone and she had caught up.

She turned on the pain box she had searched out in the brush. Wetzel froze in place, locked in sheer pain.

The other team members froze similarly. They were all immobilized by pain. They were all captive. Again. Along with MaleBug and all the female scarabs. All of them were trying to repel the poacher, but Zora's hardened immunity prevailed.

Then Wetzel rose into the air. He floated past open-mouthed Zora, who simply could not believe what she was seeing. He landed on the end of the trail, and the pain abated.

Wizard had used his levitation magic to carry Wetzel across the line, saving the day.

Then, as Wetzel watched, Zora herself floated up above head height. And abruptly dropped to the ground. The pain box flew from her hand and bounced across the terrain.

At that point the others stepped forward to join Wetzel on the trail. Veee was still carrying Wizard.

They gazed at Zora, who evidently could not see them. She was battered but not seriously hurt. And in a bewildered rage. Her recaptured prey had done something impossible, then vanished. She couldn't understand it.

"Thank you, Wizard," Vanja said.

He did not answer. Still strewn over Veee's sturdy shoulder, he was unconscious. He had given his all. When his body no longer worked, his magic had remained.

Now Wetzel truly understood why they had been so careful to preserve Wizard's full strength. Every bit of it had been required.

At last they were completely safe from the brute poachers, and so were the approximately fifty other females Wetzel carried on his coat.

They made their way along the trail toward RedBrick Village. Progress was fair, but Wetzel was increasingly uncomfortable for another reason. He needed to poop. He couldn't risk it here; he had to get to the well.

And MaleBug needs to breed. He can't wait much longer.

They came to RedBrick. Vanja flew ahead to alert the men. She returned to report that they were ready to assist in transportation. They had rounded up a horse-drawn wagon they would use to transport Wetzel to PinkPebble and the well. Also tools to remove shackles.

After that it was easier and faster. Wetzel for the first time in his life got to ride a horse-drawn wagon instead of hauling it. They reached the well, and he hurried across to put his hind end over it. He pooped voluminously. The villagers applauded. He felt the mind trace of MaleBug as the capsule emerged and dropped down into the well.

He's there! LadyBug thought. *I must follow!*

Farewell! Wetzel replied. There was so much more he wanted to say to her, but no time to say it.

He felt her mind as she flew from his head, down the well. The fifty other female scarabs followed in a cloud.

His job done, Wetzel changed to man form. He put his head over the well, hoping to receive a key thought.

And there it was. The immense bliss of seminal inflation, expanding extraordinarily, followed by sudden cessation in a literal explosion of joy.

LadyBug had won the choice. LadyBug had bred. LadyBug was no more.

Wetzel sank to the ground with mixed joy and grief. They had accomplished their mission. They had saved the precious scarab from extinction. Yet he wished he could have had LadyBug with him to stay.

Hands came to him, guiding him away. "I will cheer you to the extent I am able," Veee said. "You performed splendidly. We all know that."

"Give credit to Wizard. He saved us all in the end."

"You know what I mean. You did your vital part."

"It's the right thing," he agreed. "I am glad for LadyBug. She achieved her life's ambition. But I love her and miss her so much."

"You lost your virgin," Veee agreed. "That is one thing I can't help you with any more."

She truly understood. He turned into her, put his head against her solid shoulder, and sobbed.

———

Soon they were back in their old room in the house on PinkPebble. It was much as before, with Wizard being tended by Veee, who was now free of the manacles. The men had seen to that detail.

"When we recover," Tod said, "We shall have to consider our future as a team. Are we game for another such challenge?"

"Oh yes," Vanja said. "I love this adventurous life."

Tod smiled. "Maybe the next mission will be able to provide you with more men to seduce, so you won't have to be so sexually starved."

She smiled back. "That would be nice."

"I'm game," Veee said. "Though I don't need more sex."

They looked at Wetzel, who now had a bandage on his healing wrist. "I'm game also," he said. "I have yet to find my virgin."

There was a knock on the door. It was Pinkie. "I am here on business, after an excellent night with Red," she said. "As you know, all three of my girls who nighted with the unicorn got pregnant. Paige too; that makes four. We are now in a much better situation with respect to male company, thanks to Vanja's effort, but we still would like to keep Wetzel for our own. I am going to make him an offer he can't refuse."

Wetzel shook his head. "I have already committed to continuing with the team. I must keep searching for my virgin."

"Precisely. We have found her for you."

All of them looked at her. "We're not sure you understand Wetzel's situation," Vanja said. "He longs for a virgin he can keep. To marry and sire children by, yet have her remaining virginal throughout. No ordinary woman can do or be that. It is a paradox, his personal curse."

"Exactly. We searched and located that virgin in another village, and brought her here. Her village was glad to let her go; she is unmarriageable in the ordinary manner. Wetzel can have her, provided he agrees to settle down in PinkPebble and service any other of our girls who desire it. The roles are not incompatible."

Something was up. "Maybe I should meet this girl," Wetzel said warily.

"This way. You may night with her."

"I doubt I will need to. After the first connection my interest will wane."

"I doubt it."

"Because of my curse. No necessary fault in her. But I would not want to lead her on with expectations of marriage when that is simply not feasible."

She just smiled.

"What is her name?"

"Virginia, of course."

"What are you not telling me?"

"She doesn't remember. Not beyond a day, if that. That's why no man would marry her."

"She's an amnesiac?"

"Not exactly. She merely lacks the ability to remember events after she sleeps. It is a fault in her memory processing. She can speak, she can read, she knows the conventions of society, she can do routine chores, she knows her name. She's a nice girl. She merely can't remember personal things."

"This must be a horror for her!"

"No. She doesn't remember. Each morning someone must acquaint her anew with her situation, in a kindly manner." Pinkie faced him momentarily. "She is emotionally virginal every morning."

Wetzel paused as that sank in. Virginity for him was not really of the body, or even of the mind, but of the emotion. That novelty of first experience. "Oh, my."

"She needs someone to love her, to have the patience to brief her each day, to protect her from molestation or affront or teasing by others. She needs a man to appreciate her for what she is. We believe you can be that man."

"But if it is all gone the next day, how can there be any continuity?"

"It is too bad she can't have a telepathic scarab on her head, as I gather you did, to refresh her memory each morning. As it is, you will have to do that job. It should not be burdensome."

"I am not at all sure of that."

"Here we are. I will introduce you, then depart. In due course you may inform me of your decision." She knocked on the door.

In a moment it opened to reveal an ordinary young woman of perhaps eighteen. She had brown hair, brown eyes, a pretty face, a slender torso, and an innocent, faintly nervous expression. The essence smote him like a hammer made of air.

She was indeed a virgin. It radiated from every aspect of her.

"Pinkie!" she said gladly.

"Virginia, I have brought a man to meet you. I think he will like you, and be your friend."

"I need a friend," Virginia said. She turned her gaze on Wetzel.

"Hello."

He was already falling in love with her. "Hello, Virginia. I am Wetzel."

"Hello, Wetzel. Please come in."

He stepped into the room. She closed the door behind him, then turned to give him her full attention. She knew her manners.

Pinkie remained outside, by no coincidence; he read it in her mind as she departed. She was letting him get to know Virginia in his own fashion.

He took her hand. "I understand you do not remember yesterday."

"I do not," she agreed. "Are you from my village? Do you know me? I am sorry I do not remember you."

"I have not met you before. This is our first meeting."

"Then you do not know me any better than I know you. Will you really be my friend?" She was so plaintively hopeful. Existing without past memories was intensely lonely.

"More than that, perhaps." He took a breath. "Virginia, may I kiss you?"

"My boyfriend?" There was a flare of excitement in her mind. She wanted a serious relationship, but did not know whether she could have it. Pinkie had evidently explained about her daily loss of memory.

"I hope to be your boyfriend, yes."

"Then you may kiss me." She knew the protocol, at least to that extent. She shouldn't kiss a stranger, but could kiss a boyfriend.

He took her in his arms and gently kissed her. Her body yielded gracefully and her lips firmed. She knew how to kiss, even if she could not remember doing it before. It was delightful in its innocent novelty.

She also knows that a kiss could be a prelude to making love.

She did not know the details of that, but was willing to discover them.

There would be more, much more, but he already knew. "Virginia, will you marry me?"

She was taken aback. "Are you sure we just met?"

He had to explain. "Virginia, I am a mind reader. I know what you are thinking. I know you are the kind of woman I want to marry. I will stay with you and support you in all the ways you need. It will be easier if we are married."

"So you can have sex with me!" she exclaimed. She knew that much about marriage.

"That, too," he agreed.

That sufficed. "Yes, if it is all right with Pinkie. She told me not to make any commitments that go beyond a day without her approval."

"Pinkie wants what's best for you. I will go and ask her, and bring her back so she can tell you."

"Thank you."

"We will be back in perhaps half an hour."

"That's good."

He kissed her again, and she was more than willing. She was a virgin, but lacked the ordinary virgin's aversion to sex with him, probably because she had no memory to protect. Then he left her in her room and went searching for Pinkie, tracking her by her faint mind trace.

Pinkie was in her own room, awaiting his verdict. She was garbed for the evening, in a nightgown. He knocked, then entered. He took her in his arms, kissed her, then bore her back to her bed as her gown fell open. In moments they were amidst wild lovemaking, as she brought her expertise into play to facilitate his passion. She loved this; it was in her mind.

In due course they got up, cleaned up, and she closed her nightgown. She accompanied him to Virginia's room. No word had been spoken.

They knocked, Virginia opened, and they stepped inside. "Yes, you may marry Wetzel," Pinkie said. "He will love you and take good care of you."

"Oh, good!" Virginia hugged her, then turned to hug Wetzel. She was so innocently pleased.

Pinkie nodded. "I will make the announcement. We will start planning the wedding."

"Thank you," Wetzel and Virginia said almost together as Pinkie departed.

"You are more than welcome." Pinkie was gone. She had achieved her objective: to get him to settle in PinkPebble Village and breed their women.

Then Wetzel kissed Virginia again. "You are a virgin," he said. "I like virgins."

She was doubtful. "I don't remember. I'm not sure whether I am really—"

"You are," he said with authority. Whatever had happened with her body, and surely much had, considering the way men were, didn't matter. She was his kind of virgin.

They talked compatibly about things, such as how he could assume unicorn form. She loved that, being naturally attracted to equines. Then they settled for the night on her bed. "Are we going to?" she asked.

"Not until we are married." Because that was her culture, and he wanted to honor it even if she didn't remember details.

They slept embraced, kissing frequently, and her happiness was manifest. So was his; the aura of her virginity suffused their association.

But in the morning she woke bemused. "Am I supposed to be here? With you? Where are we? I don't remember."

He started in. "I am Wetzel. You have a condition that prevents you from remembering the past. We have agreed to marry soon. We have slept together but not been intimate; that will wait until we marry. Except for kisses." He kissed her. "We are friends, and I will take care of you. I will not allow anything bad to happen to you. I will answer any questions you have. Now we must clean up, get dressed, and get ready for breakfast."

"Thank you." The information might be new to her, but evidently there was that in her that readily understood about her condition. She was glad to have someone to guide her socially. A friend.

He took her to meet the team members. "This is my fiancée Virginia." And to her: "You don't need to remember all their names, as they will be departing in a few days. They are my friends, and wish you well."

"We do," Veee said.

It was wonderful. He had found his ideal virgin. He had everything he had wanted. Yet there was a small nagging reservation. Wetzel felt guilty for still missing LadyBug. Why couldn't he be completely happy? He knew why: he had come to depend on the added telepathic power LadyBug had provided him, the ability to send as well as read. They had collaborated so very well, and he had loved her too, his little vicarious virgin. But she was gone, and he would simply have to get used to it.

In the afternoon he took Virginia for a walk around the village, so that the women could see them together and know it was true. They already knew about his tryst with Pinkie, of course. There would be others; it was part of the deal. But Virginia was his love, his renewable virgin. She would bear his babies, and the villagers would help raise them. He was sure Virginia would be a good mother, but she would need to be reacquainted with her situation and children each morning.

Something flew up before them. It looked like a scarab. Wetzel raised his hand, and the scarab perched on it. *Hello Wetzel! Let me borrow your big mind.*

"LadyBug!" he exclaimed jubilantly, bringing her to his head. Then he remembered. "But you can't be, because—"

I am her daughter, one of a hundred, the same age she was when you associated.

"But she was thirty years old!"

Father said you might forget that time moves at ten thousand times the rate on Refuge as it does on other worlds.

"Father?"

You called him MaleBug. He told me he owes everything to you. You rescued him from the killers. You carried him safely to Refuge, along with fifty females. Now he has bred thirty of them, but he couldn't breed me because I am his daughter. I am the one who got Mother's memory of you. I had these weird fantasies of having virtual sex with a unicorn. I don't even know what a unicorn is! I came to ask Father what was wrong with me, and he said nothing, because he knew that unicorn. There is no male in Refuge to breed me or my sisters, but he told me that I could have something almost as good. I could start the recolonization of the Amoeba. Maybe even find other males from the home world. He told me where to find you. May I stay with you, Wetzel? Will you help me find more males for Refuge?

"Yes!" he exclaimed gladly. This scarab had LadyBug's memory of him! That was as close to a restoration of the original LadyBug as was feasible. Already he could feel the wound of his loss of the original LadyBug healing. His virtual virgin had returned!

Virginia looked at him questioningly.

He would have a lot of explaining to do. But for the moment this was enough. "I want you to meet another friend of mine. Her name is LadyBug, and she will help you remember each morning." He put his hand up, LadyBug flew to it, and he held the scarab toward Virginia so she could see.

"She's lovely!"

"Not just physically," he agreed. "She is a virgin too."

"Oh! I know we'll get along."

We will, LadyBug agreed.

Already the vision of their future was forming. The team would move on without him, but he and LadyBug would make other visits to Scarabia, searching for more scarabs to save, avoiding the poachers. Completing the mission they had started. It would surely be all the adventure he craved.

There was something else. "Virginia, after we are married, I will take you to meet a dear friend of mine. You won't be able to step onto her world, but I will bring her to the end of the trail to meet you. Her name is Weava, and she will like you and LadyBug and be glad for me. You will like her too."

"I'm sure I will," Virginia said.

Very sure, LadyBug echoed.

AUTHOR'S NOTE

    I had actually worked out much of the second Trail Mix novel *Beetle Juice* before I started writing the first, *Amoeba*. They were a set, to see how the notion of a changing mix of characters along a trail worked out. When I finished the first novel I took about ten days to catch up on other chores, then started in on the second.

    And immediately had a problem. I am always conscious of the needs of my readers, and try to write what they will like, in a way they can readily assimilate. Sequels are problematic because the author can't just assume that every reader has read the first novel and is clear for the second. In the bad old days of paper books—uh, let me rephrase that: in the nostalgic bygone days of physical books, distribution could be spotty, and the first novel in a series could be out of print by the time the second was published, making it impossible for a new reader to read them in order. Electronic publishing should abate that problem, but if a friend lends his electronic reader with a novel on it, it may not be the first in the series, which got deleted to make room for new books. Same problem. So I couldn't just start in where I left off; new readers would be confused by having to untangle five main characters and a situation all at once. I needed to re-introduce the characters, one by one. But then old readers would get bored, already knowing those characters and the nature of the Amoeba, and blame the author for lacking new imagination. It's a balancing act without a clear yet compelling resolution. And that's just the readers. Reviewers can be worse, and critics sometimes seem to be eagerly looking for any supposed flaw so they can trash the book without having to read the rest of it. Ask any experienced writer.

What to do? I realized that about the only way to introduce familiar characters one by one without boring the old reader was to have a new protagonist. That is, a new viewpoint character. Then the new readers would learn about the old characters as he did, and the old readers would learn about the new character as the old ones did. With luck neither new nor old readers would catch on that they were being managed. By the time they got to this Author's Note it would be too late; they would already have enjoyed the novel. No problem with reviewers; they don't read Authors Notes, being certain that they already know what's in them. Critics? There's no hope for them anyway. As the American poet Sidney Lanier put it: "Swinehood has no remedy." And so it came to be that Wetzel became the main character. I filled in his background, as telepathic were-unicorns are not common stock, then brought him into contact with the others for the main story. You know the rest.

There are a couple of elements that distinguish this novel from run of the mill junk. One is the theme of saving a threatened species from extinction, especially a bug. Many folk think that bugs exist to be stepped on. But bugs aren't all alike. The other is the particular form of

LadyBug. She is not only telepathic, she is overtly fractal, looking like the central figure of the Mandlebrot set. That is special indeed.

This has been covered glancingly in the novel, but I'll try to clarify it further here. Fractals are everywhere in geology, nature, and life. We live in a fractal world; we just didn't know it until recently. Clouds are fractal; coast lines are fractal; trees are fractal; the human body is fractal. Put so simply as to threaten accuracy, a fractal pattern is an elaboration of an existing form, endlessly extended. Any part of it resembles the rest of it; scale becomes irrelevant. Like the fleas that have smaller fleas biting them, which in turn have smaller fleas, ad nauseam, any simple pattern can have elaborations of its outline, which in turn have elaborations, and so on. The Mandelbrot set is a fractal pattern whose basic shape resembles a bug, and whose extensions become ever more intricate and ultimately beautiful. Math and art overlap wonderfully. I get drawn in again whenever I look at the Mandelbrot set, fascinated by its devious symmetry. It has been said that fractals represent half a dimension: if you have a two-dimensional picture, its fractal outline becomes longer the further the iteration proceeds, without ever quite reaching the third dimension.

So what use is it? As it turned out, fractal math helps in the design of airplanes, the understanding of global warming, medical appreciation of the human heartbeat and bloodflow through the kidneys, the special effects of blockbuster movies, cell-phone antennas, and a myriad other practical applications. So if this novel helps alert more people to the beauty and use of fractals, that's great. You can learn a lot more about them via the Internet if you're interested. Just do a Search on "Fractals" or "Mandelbrot set." If you're not amazed by those pictures, you're not the kind of reader I want to cultivate.

So if you should encounter a ladybug, take a good look at her.

She just might be a fractal scarab masquerading as a ladybug to avoid the complications that discovery of her real nature might generate. If you look hard enough to penetrate the illusion, you might see a living Mandelbrot set. If you cultivate her acquaintance, she might even lend you her telepathy. But probably not.

And a note of appreciation: for Rudy Reyes, who proofread the manuscript, catching a number of errors I had missed.

Readers interested in learning more of me and my works can visit my hipiers.com web site, where I have a monthly column, information about my books, and an ongoing survey of electronic publishers and related services. Or my new blog site, where I post tweets and assorted thoughts on this and that. piersanthonyblog. blogspot.com/.

I don't yet know whether there will be further Trail Mix sequels. That depends on the reception of the first two novels. But it's been fun getting together for these.

ABOUT THE AUTHOR

Piers Anthony has written dozens of bestselling science fiction and fantasy novels. Perhaps best known for his long-running Magic of Xanth series, many of which are *New York Times* bestsellers, he has also had great success with the Incarnations of Immortality series and the Cluster series, as well as *Bio of a Space Tyrant* and others. Much more information about Piers Anthony can be found at www.HiPiers.com.

PIERS ANTHONY

FROM OPEN ROAD MEDIA

  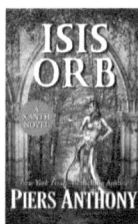

 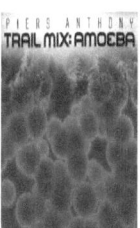  

OPEN ROAD

INTEGRATED MEDIA

OPEN ROAD

INTEGRATED MEDIA

Find a full list of our authors and
titles at www.openroadmedia.com

FOLLOW US
@OpenRoadMedia